Author's Note

P9-DNZ-350

"PRACTICE RANDOM KINDNESS AND SENSELESS ACTS OF BEAUTY"

In my city, you see this phrase scrawled on walls, illuminated on bumper stickers, and handed out in flyers. And since I've been absorbed with the concept of compassion since childhood, I've rather adopted it as my dictum. It stays in the mind and heart.

When editors at LOVESWEPT mentioned the **TREASURED TALES** theme month, I immediately thought of the fairy tale "Beauty and the Beast." In the world today we have many modern "beasts" to deal with, and compassion and kindness are the best weapons for battling the bad.

One of the most heartbreaking manifestations of the "beast" is the inability to verbalize our pain, to communicate our needs, to reach out, so that others may reach out to us. In doing that we find the most elemental of understanding, soul connections, and empathy. Without these there is isolation, depression, and defeat. With soul connections and empathy, there is freedom, choice, love.

In writing my own "Beauty and the Beast" I hope to show that one act of kindness can lead to many, that it can overpower the "beast"; and that compassion and beauty of soul are the ultimate safeguards in a society that can easily be crippled by the Hydra of poverty, disease, violence, and neglect.

Though I write for myself, dear readers, I hope you will enjoy my dabbling with one of my favorite fantasies.

Helen Mittermeyer

WHAT ARE *LOVESWEPT* ROMANCES?

They are stories of true romance and touching emotion. We believe those two very important ingredients are constants in our highly sensual and very believable stories in the *LOVESWEPT* line. Our goal is to give you, the reader, stories of consistently high quality that may sometimes make you laugh, sometimes make you cry, but are always fresh and creative and contain many delightful surprises within their pages.

Most romance fans read an enormous number of books. Those they truly love, they keep. Others may be traded with friends and soon forgotten. We hope that each *LOVESWEPT* romance will be a treasure—a "keeper." We will always try to publish

LOVE STORIES YOU'LL NEVER FORGET
BY AUTHORS YOU'LL ALWAYS REMEMBER

The Editors

Loveswept ® 588

Helen Mittermeyer
'Twas the Night

BANTAM BOOKS

NEW YORK · TORONTO · LONDON · SYDNEY · AUCKLAND

'TWAS THE NIGHT

A Bantam Book / January 1993

If you would be interested in receiving protective vinyl
covers for your Loveswept books, please write to this address
for information:

Loveswept
Bantam Books
P.O. Box 985
Hicksville, NY 11802

ISBN 0-553-44245-7

Published simultaneously in the United States and Canada

One

Winter! Alaska's glitziest season had begun. All gussied up in pure white snow that sparkled like diamonds and sapphires under the late-day sun, it put to shame all those lesser states to the south. Prince William Sound glistened, too, with the trillion priceless drops of sleet that presaged the driving, icy storm that would soon coat the snow and all of Valdez with a crystal raiment. The cold was still and stark.

Cassie Nordstrom felt the winter with an inner joy, yet with sadness as well. Eyes closed, she let Mozart burst forth on her flute, reveling in the music, needing its solace, its warm embrace. She stretched the tremolo finish of the sonata higher and higher, holding the last note before allowing it to fade into pulsating silence, then she leaned back tiredly. She'd played Mozart, Beethoven, Weber, and Schubert, filling herself with the wonder of the music she loved so much, music that had always sustained and bolstered her, given her strength when she faltered and peace when her thoughts were chaotic. She knew without looking at the clock that she'd been at it for hours. Music was her therapy, and she'd needed it badly that afternoon.

Rising, she stretched, swaying back and forth to limber her tight muscles. Sometimes she became so engrossed in her playing, she could barely move afterward. It was the price of loving music.

Walking to the window, she leaned her hot forehead against the icy pane and gazed out at the snowy panorama. This was her world for today. She'd leave Alaska tomorrow, and the trip to New York would be an uphill battle all the way. Not like the first time she'd traveled there to attend The Juilliard School, unsure and anxious, yet with her hopes and dreams burning bright. Tomorrow would be far more solemn and no less frightening.

Once more she'd be spending Christmas Eve in the Big Apple. She dreaded it even more than that first one three years ago. Not because she'd be homesick, but because she would have to face the anger of her friend Cosmo's family. And because Rafe lived there.

She closed her eyes against the pain and her greatest fear—seeing him again. She couldn't bear it. But that was ridiculous, she told herself. There'd be no reason to see him, not if she didn't want to. He didn't know she was coming, and Manhattan was huge, its concrete and glass towers and caves filled with people. And she was a woman now, not the callow girl she'd been when they first met, whose eyes had reflected the glitter of Manhattan and whose being had been filled with the wonder of first love.

"Cassie?" a man said behind her. "Cassie, girl, don't try to do this all on your own."

Brought sharply out of her reverie, she stared at her father's reflection in the glass. "I must. I promised Cosmo."

"But you're thinking of Rafe," Helborg said.

She closed her eyes. "I can't think of him now, Daddy. I have enough on my plate getting Cosmo's body back to New York and having him buried next to Raymond. And I will do it. A promise is a promise. That's priority enough."

"Yes, it is. But we had a service for him here in our church. Surely you don't need to have another out on Long Island."

"I do, Daddy. I want the same ceremony Raymond had and then they'll be just as Cosmo specified in his will. As his executor, I have the obligation to carry out his wishes."

"But I'm worried about you. Do you think Cosmo's family will even show up?"

"Who knows? They were pretty angry on the phone, but their pastor, who's saying the mass, is telling them to respect their son's last request—he told me so. Cosmo and Raymond wanted to be buried side by side. And I'll do it." She tried to smile at her father's image in the glass. "Then I'll come back to Valdez. School starts right after the first of the year. And the orchestra will need a great deal of rehearsal for the Mardi Gras festival." Teaching music was her life now, and she was happy enough. If she sometimes wondered if she could have made it as a solo performer, or even just as a member of a symphony orchestra, she didn't dwell on that. If even more often Rafe's face was in front of her mind, she'd got used to smothering the image and turning her energy to her students.

Her father put his hand on her shoulder. "I know how much your teaching job means to you. And your mother and I are glad you're back here with us, so that we can listen to your music every day. You know how I love music."

Cassie nodded. "You started me on the flute when I was in grade school, and I loved every minute of it."

"And I'm proud of what you've done and what you're doing. But I also know that you loved Rafe."

"Father, Rafe and that part of my life is over. My life is here in Alaska where I was born, not in Manhattan." And she would never see Rafe again. In the familiar pattern of pain she felt her heart squeeze in longing. Would the desire never die? Would memories of him forever blot out any chance of ever loving anyone else?

No! She wouldn't think of him. Cosmo was her focus, nothing else. She'd informed his family of his death two days earlier and that she was bringing his body back to New York so he could be buried at Raymond's side. They hadn't approved of their son's relationship with Raymond when he was alive, but they wouldn't try to stop her. She had the law on her side, and she wouldn't back down. Cosmo had made few demands of her or anyone else, but he had asked to be buried with Raymond. As executor of his will, she would honor that wish. He'd been her dear friend, her confidant, and she'd accepted the legal responsibility for carrying out his final wishes.

She still remembered the horror she'd felt that spring morning two and a half years ago, when

Cosmo had come over to see her. She'd been living with Rafe, having moved from the loft apartment she'd shared with Cosmo and Raymond to Rafe's beautiful duplex less than a month after meeting him. Raymond had died just two weeks earlier, and Cosmo's parents had arrived at his apartment the day before and seen the telltale purple blotches on his neck that told them that he, like Raymond, had contracted the plague of the twentieth century, AIDS.

Cosmo told Cassie his parents were ashamed to tell their friends—to whom they'd never even acknowledged that their son was gay—about his illness. And so they were pressuring him to commit himself to a private sanatorium upstate, even though he did not at this point require hospitalization. But they wanted to tell everyone that he'd gone abroad to further his musical career, and when the inevitable happened to pretend he'd died in Europe and have his funeral and burial sufficiently far from their home on Long Island that no one they knew was likely to discover the truth.

Cassie was appalled at the Bugassis' heartlessness. "But they can't force you to go to a sanatorium—or any of the rest of it," she reassured Cosmo.

"No, I've already been on the phone with my lawyer," he said. "He told me I could state my desire to be buried next to Raymond in my will, with instructions that my executor carry out my wishes. Raymond was my original executor, and now I'll need someone else in that capacity. Cassie, I know it's asking a lot, since my parents will probably fight you all the way, but would you—"

She interrupted to assure him she'd be his executor, and that wasn't all. Whatever turns his illness might take, Cosmo needed the care of a loving family. And if his own disowned him Cassie was prepared to offer hers. Since Rafe had been withdrawing from her emotionally, she had been thinking of returning to Valdez, to the warm circle of family and friends who would welcome her back; she knew this circle would also enfold Cosmo in its midst and offer him all the care and acceptance he craved.

Overwhelmed by her generosity, Cosmo hardly dared take advantage of it. So to persuade him, she called Valdez right then and there, putting Cosmo on the phone to hear her parents urge them to take the next plane to Alaska.

And that's just what they did. It would be easier to defy his parents from a distance, over the telephone, Cosmo reasoned, and he could get a will drawn in Valdez as easily as in New York. He would also have Cassie named his legal guardian should he become mentally incompetent, which thankfully had never happened. But she had been prepared to do whatever was necessary to ensure Cosmo's dignity for the rest of his life—and beyond.

She couldn't help but wonder now, as she had wondered then and during the long years in between, what a difference it might have made if she'd told Rafe in person, instead of in a hurried call from JFK minutes before the plane to Alaska took off. Despite the chasm between them, which had been growing ever wider for weeks, he might have reacted differently if she'd told him the whole story face-to-face. It wasn't like her to take the coward's way out, but like Cosmo, she'd dreaded a final confrontation—and perhaps, too, she'd feared losing her resolve to leave if she were even in the same room with Rafe once more.

In any case Rafe had taken the news badly. She could still recall his biting words before he'd hung up: "Thanks for all the advance notice that you're moving out. All five minutes of it."

Even though she had lost Rafe, she couldn't regret what she had done for Cosmo. Because he had contracted AIDS, his family had wanted to erase him, to hide him away until he died and even afterward. In Alaska, with her family welcoming him as a son and brother, he had lived. For a few years. Now she would not allow anything to thwart her plans to bury her friend next to Raymond.

Yet as she pondered being in Manhattan, she had to fight the trepidation that mushroomed around her. And it wasn't just Cosmo's family that had her shaking.

Rafe was in Manhattan! How would she be able to stand being that near him and not call? But if she talked to him, she'd want to see him . . . to hold him, to kiss him, to—No! What would be the sense? They'd parted, not as bitter enemies, but as coldly determined people set on divergent courses. Oh, there'd been hot, angry denunciations in those last weeks before she'd left, yet even that had not destroyed completely all the wonderful intimacies they'd shared. Even after two and a half years, her love still lived deep inside her, its flame dampened but the coals still glowing.

"Cassie, listen to me." Once again her father's voice dragged her back from her memories. "Why don't you do as Cosmo suggested and contact Rafe?"

"I—I can't, Daddy."

Helborg sighed. "I'll be right back. I'm going to get some coffee. We both need it. Then we'll talk more."

Cassie eyed the swiftly building ice storm through the cold glass. No matter how long she talked, or to whom, it wouldn't erase Rafe from her mind and heart. But she couldn't bring herself to call him. He must truly hate her. Even worse, he might have forgotten her.

That time of living with Rafe was imprinted on her mind, embossed on her heart. She'd loved him so, and almost on sight. He'd been the world to her, and she'd been positive that nothing could part them. Sighing, she pressed her cheek against the windowpane, pushing back the memories that could drown her. *Don't think of Rafe. Don't think of Rafe.*

Yet as always, despite all her resolve, she couldn't totally eradicate him from her thoughts. He was like blue flame, burning eternally. Regret twisted her smile. After all this time, Rafe was as clear in her mind as if he stood in front of her, smiling that dimpled smile that should've looked silly on such a virile man, but instead enhanced his masculinity. Was he peering at her through the frosty glass? Sometimes she had the sensation that she could see him, that he was next to her . . . that he was holding her.

"Here's your coffee, Cassie."

She started, then turned and accepted the cup from her father. "I know you're worried about me, Dad. Don't be, I'll be fine."

"Your mother and I have always known how it was for you and Rafe. You loved him. We could hear your joy each time you phoned us and he was with you. That sort of love doesn't die."

He took her arm, leading her to the sofa and urging her to sit. "Then you came home with Cosmo, your face as frozen as the tundra. You were iced over with pain and loss, and not all your devotion to Cosmo masked it, dear child." He smiled sadly. "We knew that you loved Cosmo Bugassi like a brother. That's why you brought him to us when he became ill with AIDS. We also knew that you left your great love behind you in New York."

She took her father's hand, squeezing it. "But I'm better now." And she was. Sometimes she'd go for hours and not think of Rafe. "Please don't worry about me. I promised Cosmo I would bury him next to Raymond, and I will." She tightened her grip on her coffee mug. "No matter what his family says about it."

"Then let me go with you," Helborg said.

She shook her head. "I have to do this myself." She smiled wryly. "After all, I'm Cosmo's executor."

More than that, though, Cassie knew her father couldn't spare the money to fly to Manhattan. After the oil spill on Prince William Sound, he and other fishermen had been landlocked. Without his fishing trade he hadn't been able to support his small fleet of boats. Ultimately he'd been forced into bankruptcy. Her parents had managed to keep their home, but most of their other assets had disappeared a lot faster than the oil. She wouldn't allow him to extend himself any further.

Her marginal salary as a music teacher at the local junior high didn't allow for many extras, but she'd saved for the day when she'd have to return to New York with Cosmo's body. She had just enough money to cover her own expenses.

"I hope you don't meet Cosmo's parents, Cassie. They haven't forgiven you for what you did. Your care for the son they tried to hide away puts them to shame. Their letters spell that out rather plainly." He sighed. "I fear for you, Cassie, but I understand your commitment."

She smacked one fist into her palm. "Cosmo was my dearest friend. Should I have let them stick him in some sterile, lonely sanatorium?" When her father shook his head, tears sprang to her eyes. "He lived for almost three years, Daddy. At that sanatorium he would've died of loneliness in a few months. Here, he had a family, visitors, and every day he played the flute, almost until the end. Look at how he took up sculpting and painting. He did beautiful work. He lived happily until he died. He loved all of you."

"And we loved him. But we know what a sacrifice you made, what a great love you abandoned."

She looked away, fighting the grief that always threatened to engulf her when she remembered Rafe. "Maybe my love abandoned me, Dad."

Helborg touched her cheek with a work-roughened hand. "I loved your mother from the moment I saw her, but I made mistakes with her. I could've lost her." He sighed. "You should remember that, my dearest star."

Cassie shook her head. "No, Dad, you couldn't have lost Mother. You and Mother were made to be together." And she wasn't destined to spend a life with Rafe. Their inability to truly share, to truly touch each other's hearts in their months together, proved that. As swiftly as their passion had grown, and as quickly as Cassie had fallen in love with him, she'd never known if he loved her. He said he did, yet she'd always sensed a reticence in him, an unnatural suppression of any fiery emotions. Whenever problems arose between them, he would seem to ice over, flatly stating his case and leaving her to agree with him or drop it. Hurt and confused by his withholding parts of himself from her, she retaliated by withdrawing herself. Their estrangement grew so bad, she wasn't sure they even talked to each other during those last days together.

What was he doing now? she couldn't help wondering. He was thirty-four. Was his business still successful? Did he still live in the same apartment, which had been professionally decorated and which she'd thought had all the personality of a hotel room? Was he married?

Helborg touched her arm. "You're thinking about him now, aren't you?"

She nodded, swallowing her tears. "I'll be fine. I'll be just fine."

Her father's answering smile was tinged with skepticism. "You met Rafe on Christmas Eve," he said softly. "And you'll be in Manhattan on Christmas Eve again."

"Manhattan is huge, Daddy, filled with bustling, hustling people. I'm more obscure there than I'd be out in the Alaskan wilderness."

That night as she lay in bed, Cassie tried not to think of Manhattan, the time when she and Cosmo and Raymond were all enrolled in the graduate program at Juilliard—she and Cosmo played the flute, Raymond the trombone—and Rafe was the joy in her life. Still, it all broke over her like a tidal wave, the memories crashing crystal-clear around her. It seemed a lifetime ago. It seemed like yesterday. And not all her struggling to forget could blot out the bittersweet memories of her first love.

Two

Snow swept over everything with white paws, dappling the sidewalk, dusting coats, hats, and bare heads, creating a soft kitten-cover over the busy metropolis of Manhattan. Cassie wandered along Fifth Avenue amid hundreds of last-minute shoppers and celebrants. She felt weary and sad and not at all festive.

Cosmo had been buried that morning, and the funeral service had been a strain. Despite their threats, his parents had been there, and she had shivered at the animosity they'd directed at her. But she'd got through it, and they hadn't interfered. Cosmo had been buried next to Raymond in the small cemetery out on Long Island.

Back in the city, she'd changed clothes in her small hotel room.

Feeling closed in by the four walls, she'd donned a jacket and boots and decided to window-shop on Fifth Avenue. It was, at least, miles from Greenwich Village, where she had first met Rafe Brockman three years ago that night. Reason told her she'd never see him; she was flying back to Alaska the next day. Yet she strolled down the avenue, she didn't feel the bite of winter wind, the touch of snow on her face. All she felt was Rafe. Surrounded by millions of people, she felt only Rafe. She needed him so much.

On impulse she strode to the nearest corner, joining the other pedestrians waiting there to cross Fifth Avenue. She'd go to Rockefeller Center and watch the skaters. She and Rafe had skated there. She'd known then she loved him.

She couldn't help recalling that Christmas Eve three years ago when she'd been marooned in Manhattan, unable to afford the airfare to go home for the holidays and aching with loneliness for the crisp white blankets of snow in Valdez. Traditional carols would bell up into the navy-blue star-riddled sky from all the friendly churches, and people would smile and wave because they knew her. No one knew her in New York except her fellow students at Juilliard.

She'd been making extra money playing in the pit orchestra for an off-Broadway show. They'd had an early performance that Christmas Eve, and when it was over, she'd rushed out, eager to return to her apartment and wait for her parents to call. In her haste she'd rammed into a man. Actually she'd hit him between the legs with her flute case. His rather bored-sounding "Pardon me" still tinkled in her memory like the Christmas bells.

"Hey, lady, you crossin'? The light's green."

Cassie jerked, startled from her reverie by the impatient, gift-laden man trying to get past her.

"Oh. Sorry." She moved to one side, stepping off the curb. Feeling sad and joyous, poignantly hugging and desperately eschewing yesterday's memories, she crossed Fifth Avenue. She watched faces, wondering where the different people were going, whom they'd see, when they'd sit around the Christmas tree exchanging gifts. Her favorite holiday of the year and she was alone again. She fought the rising sense of desolation and let her mind take her back again to Rafe.

She'd stammered an apology about hitting him in such a vulnerable spot. "It's easier to carry with a shoulder strap," she'd explained.

"Tough on passersby," he'd said. "Good weapon, though."

Then they'd laughed, and she had fallen in love.

Love, Cassie thought. Cosmo had taught her so much about loving, about not wasting a moment of that precious gift given to only a few. In one of their last conversations he'd talked about it again.

"Love, Cass, that's what counts. I want you to promise me you'll find Rafe and tell him you love him."

That thought was almost frightening, and she'd tried to make light of it. "What if he throws me out on my ear?"

Cosmo hadn't let her get away with that. "Then you tackle him and tie him down, make him see, force him to understand. I want you to be happy, Cass. Promise me you will."

"I promise."

Cassie sighed as she walked slowly down the concourse toward the skating rink. She'd made that promise three weeks ago, and had yet to keep it. She'd had hundreds of excuses, though she knew the real reason was her fear that Rafe wouldn't even remember her name. She stopped dead, realizing how ridiculous she was being. She'd promised Cosmo she'd call Rafe, and if she were honest with herself, she'd admit that she longed to hear his voice. She would keep that promise. She'd call Rafe right now. Whirling around, she bumped smack into someone. "I'm so—"

Strong arms took hold of her. "'Twas the night before Christmas . . .'"

The voice whispered above her head, repeating the words Rafe had said that long-ago Christmas. If he hadn't been holding her, she would've sagged to the icy pavement.

"Rafe?" she said weakly, gazing up at him. "Is it you? Is it really you?"

"In the flesh." His grip tightened. "Whenever I think of you, that phrase goes through my mind. That first Christmas Eve I thought you were an elf, a five-foot-eight-inch one. Your beautiful hair was caught up under a wool cap, and you were bundled up like an Eskimo. All I could see of your face was your wide-apart eyes and your prominent cheekbones, and I knew before you told me that you had a Nordic background."

Cassie's ears were ringing. Was that really Rafe standing in front of her, talking to her? What had he said? "This is a very rare coincidence," she managed to say as she stared hungrily at him. He hadn't changed, except that the streaks of gray in his hair were wider, more silver. He still made her think of a modern-day warrior, Celtic dark, sensual, exciting . . . Three years ago she'd wondered if he'd been a Greek god in another life. That would explain his devastatingly harsh-handsome features. And he would've been a dangerous god. She'd thought so three years ago. She hadn't changed her mind.

"How's that?" he asked.

"What?" Disoriented by the present mixing around with the past, she'd lost track of what they'd both said.

"That this is a very rare coincidence," he whispered, his hands still holding her upper arms and bringing her closer by degrees.

"You being here. Me deciding to call you." Speaking was a struggle. She couldn't seem to get enough air. Rafel Brockman in front of her, in Manhattan. Joy mixed with wariness, happiness tossed with pain.

He stared down at her for long seconds. "It's no coincidence, Cass. Surely you must know that. You were going to call me?"

"Yes."

"Soon?"

"As soon as I found a phone." She stared at his sudden bright smile. "Tell me about the coincidence." He still had the power to make her want him, she realized, and her wariness heightened.

"It isn't one, Cass. Figure it out."

She shook her head. "I don't know if I can. Or if I want to." Cosmo was right, love was all-important. She knew that. But she wasn't sure she had the courage to face the pain of renewing their relationship. It had almost killed her to leave him the first time. Of course, she didn't know if Rafe even wanted to resurrect their love. Perhaps he was just being kind on Christmas.

"You're thinking of the past." He lifted one hand

to brush the snowflakes from her brow. "I've always loved your hair, your face," he said absently. "Don't let what was wrong with us blind you to what was right, Cass."

She tried to smile. "Hard to separate them. They were all mixed together."

He moved her to the side so that they were out of the mainstream of people wandering among the shops. He opened his mouth, then closed it again and smiled ruefully. "Maybe we could discuss that at greater length. What do you think?"

"We could do that," she said cautiously. "You look the same." Only more gorgeous, more powerful.

"You're more beautiful."

For long moments they stared at each other, and the rest of the city disappeared.

"Do you still play the flute?" he asked. "Practice every day?"

"Yes," she said shyly.

"I liked hearing you play. You were very good."

Again they were still, caught in the web of yesterday. Hands moved toward each other, then pulled back. Heads tilted, then froze. Need was palpable, a great throbbing between them.

"We need to talk, Cass."

"Yes."

He looked past her at the stairs that led down to the rink. "Why don't we skate for a time as long as we're here?"

"Are you putting me off?"

He paused, his smile twisted, then he shook his head. "Never again."

The words had been a mere wisp of sound, but they resonated through her as though a bell had clanged on each syllable. "I guess we have to take time with each other."

"And now would be good. While we skate."

"Or after."

"We might not have much time this evening. My aunt and sister are joining us for dinner and the midnight mass at Saint Patrick's."

Shaken, Cass pushed back from him. "Don't tease. I don't have a sense of humor about—"

He gently pulled her back, then turned, his arm around her, and steered them down the wide steps. "I'm not joking. We'll have dinner first, then open one gift as is the custom in Valdez among the Nordstroms."

She looked up at him. "It's been years, but you talk as though it were yesterday." And yesterday had been painful.

He grinned lopsidedly. "Yesterday is today, Cassiopeia." He pulled her closer to his side when a gust of frigid wind sliced past.

At the bottom of the stairs they stared at the rink.

"Do you remember when we first skated?" he asked.

"On Christmas Day," she whispered. "I didn't know you were going to join Cosmo, Raymond, and me." She could recall her joy when he'd appeared.

"Do you remember how suspicious Cosmo was of me?"

"Yes." And she remembered, too, the beautiful night before, Christmas Eve when it had been just the two of them, meeting for the first time, laughing, amazed at the instant rapport, delighted in both the conversation and the lengthy silences.

"After we'd skated, you invited us to eat with you. And Cosmo said we'd take the bus, even when you told him you had a car."

Rafe chuckled. "He and Raymond were very protective of you."

"Two fellow musicians. Who would need more protection than that?"

"True."

They gazed at each other, awash in the memory.

"We've lost too many yesterdays, Cassie. No more."

He sounded so grim, so determined. She wanted to respond, but she didn't know if she'd laugh or cry. Then she felt the dampness on her cheeks. It was so unreal. Rafe beside her, as though they'd never been parted. It was a Christmas miracle. Beneath her happiness, though, was the realization that the hard core of pain that had separated them was still intact. Being together could necessitate dredging it all up again.

As though in a dream she took the skates proffered by the attendant, sat down, and began to lace them. "If this is one of those strange happenings that occur in a dream, I hope someone wakes me before I freeze to death," she muttered.

"It's no dream, love. I've been watching you for two and a half years. I couldn't wait any longer to talk to you." He chuckled at her agape mouth. "C'mon, we're going to skate."

"You'd better explain first. . . . Yipes! I almost fell." He had lifted her to her feet, and aimed her toward the rink. Her knees had turned to jelly.

"I won't let that happen, Cass." He put his arm

around her and began the easy, waltzing gait that carried them smoothly around the rink.

Dozens of skaters filled the rink, while high above them many more people watched. Laughter and happy faces abounded in the charged atmosphere of Rockefeller Plaza. If now and then Cassie saw sadness etched on features, she could identify with that. Hadn't she been alone and blue not seconds before Rafe had spoken to her? Much like that first Christmas Eve, a million years ago. Or was it yesterday? Could they start fresh and new, forgetting the past?

As though she'd been pulled up by a short string, her mind rebelled against that hope. The past couldn't just be wiped away, erased as though it were a blackboard with too much writing on it. Caution mixed with her delight, and she stumbled.

Rafe instantly tightened his hold on her. "What is it? Are you cold?"

"No, no, I'm fine."

When he glanced down at her, he seemed to read her thoughts. "Don't throw it away, Cass. Not yet. We have to take baby steps. I agree on that. But I couldn't wait any longer to see you."

She looked up at him, the crisp late-afternoon air whipping back her hair as she tried to smile. "I guess I can't close the door on anything on Christmas Eve."

"Right."

His hot gaze burned through her icy doubts. Had it been so great missing him every day? she asked herself. It'd been a ride on the river Styx in a leaky boat. Cosmo had told her what a fool she'd been not contacting Rafe. Cosmo . . . She had to tell Rafe about Cosmo.

"Rafe . . . Cosmo's dead." Air caught in her throat, and she couldn't look at him. "It was quick at the end. He slipped into a coma and died the next day." She bit her lip to still its trembling. "I brought his body back for burial here, next to Raymond."

Rafe kept skating. "I know. I was at the service out on the Island. Very beautiful, very moving. He would've liked it."

She almost fell again. "I never saw you."

"I wasn't sure you'd want to, so I stayed out of sight." He smiled. "Those Gothic columns are great for hiding behind. I fully intended to drive you back, but then you took the train."

"I wouldn't have minded you being there. Cosmo liked you."

"Not at first. He glowered at me all the time we skated on Christmas Day."

She chuckled, remembering how both Cosmo and Raymond had seen fit to give her fatherly advice about Rafe. They skated on in silence, until Cassie suddenly looked up at Rafe.

"How did you know about Cosmo?"

He shook his head. "That's another thing I have to tell you. For now, we'll skate."

And they did. Swooping, swirling, dipping, weaving to the music. For a moment they could be just two ordinary people caught up in the wonder of the season, on a sweet, festive plane, basking in the crisp goodness of the holiday time.

As the sky darkened and Cassie's feet started to get cold, they finally left the ice. They walked toward Sixth Avenue side by side, but Cassie felt the distance of years of unanswered questions between them.

They'd no sooner stopped at the curb when a taxi materialized in front of them. They always did that with Rafe, Cassie thought with amusement. She'd often wondered if you had to be born in New York to have that facility. All the time she'd spent there, she hadn't been able to solicit a ride without rigorous aerobic darting, weaving, and waving. Rafe did it with a glance.

The rattle, bang, bang of the taxi, the spiraling snow, the heated interior with its stale scent of former riders compressed over them. Cassie stood the silence for a minute, then waded in, over her head at once. "So, you knew I was coming to Manhattan?"

"Yes."

"How?"

"Cosmo."

Her head snapped his way. "What?"

"Cosmo began calling me almost from the moment he arrived in Valdez."

"But . . . my father . . . mother . . . I would've known."

"Your father knew. In fact, I had to argue with him about paying for Cosmo's calls. He's one tough man."

Cassie nodded, swallowing a sob. "He loved Cosmo, treated him like a son."

"You miss him."

"Oh, yes. I'll always miss one of the best friends anyone could ever have. He taught me about compassion, courage, the ability to face adversity and come up smiling. And I'll always hear his laughter in my heart."

"He taught me the same things," Rafe said.

"What do you mean?"

He slanted a crooked smile at her. "We can save that until we're home."

At his comment she sat up straight and looked around. "This isn't the way to my hotel."

He drew a deep breath, watching her intently. "We're not going to your hotel."

"I see." The old familiar ire floated up from the depths of her being. Rafe had the bad habit of making decisions for her. She turned to him, expecting the usual closed look on his face when he expected trouble from her. He was grinning! "What is it? Why are you looking that way?"

"I'm not backing away from any more of our battles, lady. I'm going to meet you head-on."

"A veritable clash of Titans," she murmured. "What happened to you? Did you go into therapy or something?"

As soon as she spoke, she realized how rude she sounded. She'd meant it as a jest, partly. After all, he did seem different. But the comment had come out wrong, more like an insult. Had she closed another door between them with her thoughtless remark?

"Rafe," she said quickly, as if she saw the chasm yawning between them once more. "Forgive me. I know how it must've sounded, and I—"

"It's a hard question," he interrupted. "But fair." He looked out the window as though the flashing street scene held all his focus. "I did talk to a friend of mine in the field. She recommended several sessions. I went. They helped."

Cassie could feel his pain, like a thousand tiny

knife slices in his being. He swallowed as though a rock had been lodged in his throat. "I know it cost you greatly to say that," she whispered.

He shot her a sharp look. "Yes. But I did say it."

She stared at him. "You're not angry with me."

"Don't sound so stunned, darling." He grimaced. "I must've been hell to live with."

"Only at times." Relief was a river in her. "Of course, when I was winning our arguments, it didn't seem too bad."

He laughed out loud.

She felt him move closer, and it was all she could do to hold back. Throwing herself into his arms seemed like the only sensible move. How had she lived without him for so long?

Her anger gone, she asked the cab to make a quick detour to her hotel so she could retrieve her luggage, and Rafe made no objection. After that the cab continued on to its original Fifth Avenue destination. When it stopped, Rafe paid the cab-driver as the doorman of his building hurried out to open the door. He took her two small cases. Rafe eased out, then turned to her, hands outstretched.

She hesitated, looking up at him.

"You were always a gambler, Cass. Remember how we met?" When she nodded, he grinned. "Take a chance on me now."

She put her hands in his, and he caught her up, lifting her clear of the piles of gray snow, soiled from street sprays and splashes.

The cab drove away, and still he held her, studying her.

"We must make quite a picture," she said, smiling.

"New York has seen it all," he murmured, his mouth touching hers. He let her slide down his body, then his hands swept over her, adjusting her coat, retying her scarf. "Cold."

"Not bad." Her insides were jelly because all her long dreams of night were materializing. Rafe was real. He was here in front of her. And they were going to talk, not slide over the issues, argue, or ignore them. Had he really meant it?

"I can see doubts in your eyes, Cassie."

She sighed. "I have some."

"So do I. But we can talk about it." He paused. "Why are you smiling?"

"That word. Talk. That wasn't in our vocabulary before."

"It is now." He took her arm. "I think you'll like the changes."

"What changes?" she asked when they were in the elevator. His grin was so boyish, so carefree, she thought. Was this the Rafe she knew? Her heart wrenched. She wanted the changes, but she didn't want the man she'd loved so desperately to disappear entirely.

"You'll see."

The elevator stopped, and its doors opened onto the spacious foyer of Rafe's apartment.

Cassie stepped out, smiling, then the smile froze. The stark white walls, the large diamond-shaped black-and-white tile floor, the Daliesque artwork, were gone. In their place were pale peach walls with cream wainscoting and ceiling trim, a wood floor of wide random-width oak. Against one wall was a Louis XV lowboy, and the beveled mirror above it reflected the warm colors, giving the area space and a coy beckoning. Overhead was a crystal chandelier, tulip shaped, and welcoming. The staircase to the second floor was no longer a wrought-iron banister and steps with open treads. It was a master of woodworking, the treads closed and with a Persian runner down the center of them. The focal point of the foyer was a large and most beautiful oval Persian rug in apricot, coral, green, and cream. Cassie was overcome. The colors, the furnishings, were her favorites. It was her kind of room.

"It's—it's incredibly warm and welcoming."

"I thought you'd like it," Rafe said from behind her. He brushed a kiss against her hair, then walked around her and began unfastening the buttons of her wool coat.

Cassie shook. Her hands and arms felt like lead, yet she had the sensation she could fly. She felt alive, shy and yet sure. She was with Rafe. On Christmas Eve . . . again. She wanted to laugh, to cry, to run, to stay. She noticed the Christmas tree in the corner. "You have gold and peach decorations. How festive they are. It looks like an understated Versailles." She bit her lip. "I don't mean that it looks ostentatious—"

"I know." He pushed a button, and part of the mirrored wall behind her opened to reveal the closet. He hung her coat next to his.

The simple gesture seemed so familiar, so intimate, she caught her breath. She tried to smile but couldn't keep her lips from trembling. "So that's where the closet went. What a good idea."

"Modern technology."

"Astute carpentry."

He grinned. "Welcome home, Cassie."

She stepped back. "Rafe, I—"

"Relax, Cass." He took her hand and turned to the stairs. "Come and see our suite."

She hesitated, glancing up the stairs, then at him.

He looked back at her. "Don't, Cassie. I don't want you to fear me, or what you think I might've planned. It was a slip. I meant my room. You'll have your own room."

She looked away from him. "I know it's silly." If he knew how much she wanted to rush him up those stairs and into bed . . .

"It isn't silly. It's been three years." He tugged her hand, bringing her alongside him. "Step by step. Any speed you want."

She nodded and climbed the stairs with him. Had he been talking about them, their life and future, when he said "step by step"? She was both thrilled and terrified at the thought. When her hip bumped his thigh, heat radiated through her. Did he know that she'd give all she had to climb into his big bed once more and welcome him into her arms? She couldn't stem the shiver of want.

His arm went around her, and he looked down at her. "You trembled. Did you catch a chill at the rink? I'll get you a hot drink."

"No, I'm fine. Really."

On the landing she paused, memories washing over her. How many times had they climbed those stairs, whispering, laughing, eager for the love-making that was moments away? It seemed only hours ago, not years.

She heard a door close along the hall and turned. Recognizing the stocky majordomo striding toward them, she smiled. "Is that you, Buster Dunn?"

"Jeeves is the name," he said brusquely, and her smile widened. She'd teased the man about his affected use of the name Jeeves, until he finally told her his real name. "You've been gone too long," Buster added, prying her away from Rafe and hugging her. "I didn't like it."

Neither did I. The words almost popped out of her mouth. "Thank you. I've missed you too. Do you still make the best bouillabaisse in town?"

"Certainly." Buster eyed Rafe. "Got smart, did ya?"

"Yes."

"Thought you'd better get a move on." Buster chuckled when Rafe glared at him. "And don't bother firing me again. Your aunt's here. I'll go to her."

"Don't think she'll save you," Rafe said.

"Oh, but I know she will. Miss Adela likes me. So does Miss Linnie." Buster winked at Cassie, then started back to the stairs. "I've got a few more things to ready for the Christmas meal, so if you'll excuse me, Miss Cassie. Dinner's at seven. Merry Christmas."

"The same to you." Cassie stared after him as he hurried down the stairs. "He mentioned your sister and aunt."

"Yes."

"They're staying here?"

Rafe nodded. "It's Christmas Eve, the night traditionally given over to welcoming friends and relatives."

"Is it, indeed?" All those months she and Rafe were together, he'd made it quite clear that he preferred they be alone. He'd evaded talking about his sister and aunt, let alone having them for dinner. She'd never met them.

He took her arm again, and they moved down the hall.

"You've wallpapered," she said. "It's very bright and fresh." She was nervous, and preferred studying the walls to looking at him.

"Thank you." He stopped and opened a door. "Here's your suite."

She looked into the room. "Oh, my," she breathed. Again the room was done in peach and apple-green hues. The bed was huge and square with a headboard of cream satin and a down coverlet in peach. "It's lovely." She wandered around the room, reveling in its warmth, then faced him. "You've certainly done a great deal of renovation."

"Yes. And I must say I like the result. Do you?"

"Yes. Why?"

He stared at her for a long moment, then walked over to the window that looked down on Central Park. "I didn't want to waste any more time. I thought three years was plenty."

She swallowed. "I see."

"Not yet, but you will." He turned back to her. "I can tell you part of it, if you'd like to listen."

She wanted to, but she was still afraid. If she was to bolster herself against another parting from Rafe, she'd need all her armor. She would not drape herself over him and beg him to love her again.

"What are you thinking?" He crossed the room to her and slipped one arm around her waist. "I've missed you." He kissed her cheek, then stepped back, as though he'd changed his mind about talking with her, opening up to her. "Your bags are here, and I'm sure you'll find everything you need. If not, ring for Jeeves." He whirled and was gone.

Cassie blinked at the sudden emptiness of the room, at the acute aloneness without him. "How do I handle life without you, Rafe?"

Why handle it?

"I'm not listening to voices." She put her hands over her ears.

You'd better. You could lose him altogether.

"What do you suggest? Throwing him to the ground and pinning him?"

No, but you could tell him up front that you love him and need him.

"Hah! You think that's easy?"

The woman standing in the doorway listened to Cassie's one-way conversation for a moment, then arched her neck so that she could see around the half-open door. No one. "Uh-hum. Pardon me."

Cassie spun around, red rising from her ankles, filling her neck and face. "Sorry."

"Don't be sorry, dear. I often talk to myself. But I don't seem to get as firm and sure answers as you were getting."

Cassie stared at the tiny woman with fluttery hands. "Are you Aunt Adela?"

"Guilty." She smiled brightly. "I'm the artist in the family. I give artwork to everyone, and I'm sure they throw it out. I would," she added cheerily. "It's awful."

"Is it?" Cassie was dumbfounded. Not in a million years would she have imagined this woman as Aunt

Adela. In her mind Rafe's aunt had been an imposing, even pompous, lady, tall and well built like him, with a strong mind and strong views, conscious of who she was on the human scale—high and untouchable.

The woman in front of her was petite, mischievous, elflike. It wasn't an act. Was it?

"Oh, yes. But I keep doing it."

"Pardon me." Cassie blinked, trying to recapture her place in the conversation.

"My art is awful," Aunt Adela said carefully, her voice raised a notch. "Do you read lips, dear?"

"What? Oh, yes . . . That is, no. I'm not hearing-impaired," she said lamely.

"Ah, nod off in conversations, do you? I understand. I was just telling you how poorly I draw and paint."

"I'm sure . . . you don't."

"Oh, but I do. Must do something to stir up my third and fourth cousins. Sticks, all of them. May I come in?"

"Of course." Cassie stepped back as the tiny creature swept past her, her gaze darting every which way, her small nose quivering as though on scent. "Oh, you've still to unpack. I'll help."

"Oh, really, I can do it."

"Tut, tut, my dear, it's no problem."

Cassie watched for a moment as the energetic little woman unsnapped the two small cases. Then, resigning herself to company, she tackled one of the cases, carrying her toiletries into the bathroom while Adela hung her clothes in the closet. Since she'd planned for a very short stay, she'd brought little with her.

The unpacking took only minutes, then Rafe's aunt touched Cassie's arm.

"I just wanted to welcome you back," she said. "I hope you'll stay."

"Thank you."

"Rafe will be able to tell you now, my dear."

"Tell me what?"

"About his pain. He's suffered enough." She sighed and started for the door.

"Wait," Cassie said, following her. "Please tell me what you mean."

Adela glanced back and smiled at her. "Rafe will do that. And then it won't matter so much anymore. He'll figure out I've been here, anyway. He's always been too bright for his own good." With that she left, quietly shutting the door behind her.

Cassie stared at the closed door, feeling pulled from her moorings, unanchored. According to his aunt, Rafe had suffered. She loved a man who'd paid an awful price for living. But Adela hadn't told her what it was. She said Rafe would do that. But would he? He'd never been open about his family, or anything that troubled him.

She didn't know how long she stood there, but finally she shook herself out of her musings and glanced at her watch. It was time to dress for dinner. Like an automaton, she went to the closet, opened it, and pulled out the first outfit she touched. Frowning, she stared at the gown. She hadn't picked the dress she'd brought from Valdez, but a gown that had been in the closet all along. It was one Rafe had bought her. When she'd left him, she'd left most of her clothes, not because he'd bought them for her, but because she'd been on the run and wanted to take only what she could easily carry. This dress and all the other beautiful clothes carried a special baggage of their own. If she'd taken them to Valdez, they would've flooded her with all she was trying to smother, just as this gown did now. She felt drowned in a want, a need for Rafe!

The gown was made of pale tangerine silk and was starkly plain, falling straight from the one-shoulder bodice to the floor. Still, it was undeniably sophisticated, and the silk, she remembered, had a tendency to cling to the curves of her breasts and hips. She'd bought shoes to go with it, sandals made from a dull gold leather with a low heel and narrow straps.

Placing the gown on the bed, she went back to the huge closet, pushing aside other garments to look into the shoe organizer. It was capacious enough to hold a hundred pairs, but now was mostly empty. There they were!

Putting the shoes next to the bed, she studied the gown again, wondering if she had the nerve to wear it. She never heard the knock on the door, or the door opening.

"Beautiful. And your color."

The female voice had a deep whiskey tone, though the words were flat, ironic. Cassie turned, her smile wary. "Hello."

"Hello. I'm Linnie. And you're Cassie."

"Yes." Rafe's sister, Cassie thought, unable to keep from staring. Linnie Brockman was stunningly beautiful. Her dark straight hair hugged her face like a hood of ebony silk. Understated makeup enhanced her porcelain skin and large gray eyes, eyes that seemed oddly old in that lovely face.

"Your aunt was just here."

"Really? Dragging out the skeletons?"

"No. Greeting me."

Linnie inclined her head, her smile fleeting. "Ah, well then, so do I. Merry Christmas, and welcome to our home."

She had her brother's brittle reserve, Cassie thought. "Thank you. Merry Christmas to you."

"Nice to get the amenities behind us." Linnie pulled out a cigarette pack and eyed it for a long moment. "I'm trying to quit. Looking at these things and realizing I'm paying to make myself ill sometimes works. I still crave them, though." She shoved the pack back into the pocket of her deep red silk pants.

"I smoked for about a month when I was in high school. I stopped because it interfered with my playing."

"Yes, you're a flutist. Rafe told us. I wish you'd play for us sometime. I love music."

"Then you'd love my family. They all bang away at instruments and sing."

Linnie's smile was more natural. "Sounds like fun."

"It is."

"Maybe I'll get to Alaska one day."

"Come to Valdez any time. There's always room."

"Thanks. I guess I'll see you at dinner."

"Yes."

The two women gazed at each other a moment longer, and Cassie felt a strange connection with Rafe's younger sister. It was as though Linnie had something to tell her, but couldn't. She'd had the same sensation with Adela.

After Linnie left, she took a shower. When she

came out of the bathroom, Rafe was sitting on her bed, leaning back against the mound of pillows. "Hello," she said, wondering if anyone in this household ever waited to be invited into a room.

"Hello."

"Is something wrong?"

"Yes, but not with us. We have a little time before dinner. I'd like to tell you something."

She stiffened.

He swung his feet to the floor. "Shall I dry your hair?"

"I—"

"Let me."

All of their yesterdays crashed around her when Rafe unwound the towel from her head and urged her down onto the dressing-table stool. How many times had he done that when they lived together? She closed her eyes and forgot everything but the joy of being with him.

Three

Rafe watched Cassie's face in the mirror as he gently combed her hair. Her eyes were closed, and she seemed lost in some sensual dream. His own body was tightening with desire. How many times had he dried her hair for her, then ended up making love to her?

As if she'd read his mind, Cassie started, her eyes flying open. Their gazes met in the mirror, and he saw her uneasiness.

He leaned over her. "Shh, darling. Nothing is going to happen unless you want it."

"Too soon," she said weakly.

"All right." He stroked her hair, feeling the surge of heat that her nearness always brought. "But I'd have more if I could. I still want you." He grinned at her in the mirror. "And you still blush easily."

"Only because you're so blunt."

"I'm trying to be more open with you." His grin widened. "But I guess I can tone down the frankness."

"Please do."

He wanted to keep her at ease, but he couldn't stifle the clear memory of the first time they made love. They'd laughed when he'd carried her up the stairs. She'd kissed his cheek. He'd held her close. And their words were breathy, sexy, eager, unsure.

"So, tonight," she murmured, "we'll have sweet music, candlelight, silk sheets—"

"Would you believe satin, Cassie?" He reddened when she hooted with laughter. "Crazy, huh? I shopped for them myself."

In the bedroom he let her slide down his body, kissing her over and over, his heart beating out of rhythm as she kissed him back, openmouthed, eager.

They moved to the bed together, sitting on it. She looked away, and he saw her shyness. "I won't hurt you, darling."

"I know." Reaching up, she unbuttoned his shirt. "Undress me, Rafe," she said huskily.

At first it was slow. Just a tasting of each other. A nibble of the ear, a peck on the nose, a slow tracing of cheek and jaw. Fingers twined with fingers, then released to make a path of discovery, a warm way from ankle to neck.

In minutes they were skin to skin, dispatching their clothes with all speed. He felt awkward, unfledged with her, wanting her so much he was trembling, but wanting her pleasure more than his own. He'd never felt such a deluge of emotion, been swamped by such a river of sensation. He was adrift with no way to find anchor or purchase, shocked at her ability to pull him apart.

The kisses between them went from intense sweetness to flaming passion.

Cassie gasped with its power, her fingers digging into his shoulders. In hot acceptance she slanted her mouth across his, giving him access even as she greedily demanded more of his heat.

When Rafe felt her tremors begin, he held her closer, his hands and mouth urging her to fulfillment. Having her and giving himself to her was a joy he'd not dreamed he could experience.

"Darling, darling!"

She burned him, carried him in flames to the stars, until he was flying, falling free, unencumbered, light.

"There's no one but you." The words were torn from him, but they were true. In those moments she'd become his life.

All through that wonderful night of love, they murmured sweet things, hot, wanting words. Not once did they say, "I love you."

"Rafe? Rafe, you're daydreaming. I've never seen you do that." Cassie was caught between amusement and the frightening knowledge that she didn't want to be anywhere but with him. Not just on her favorite holiday, but on all days of the year, the good and the bad, the happy and the sad. "I'm seeing a new side of you."

"There's more, Cass. You'll know it all. Nothing held back." He exhaled slowly, his hand caressing the drying, shining strands of her hair, the ends curling around his finger. "I have a story to tell you."

She stiffened, knowing instinctively that what he was going to say had great import, and that it would hurt him to say it. Would it be her pain too? "Go on."

He put the comb down and turned her to face him. Kneeling before her, he clasped her arms, rubbing gently. "This is not a pretty tale. And it should've been forgotten. I thought I had forgotten it, but I've discovered that I'd just tamped down the bitterness, not buried it. Now, I intend to eradicate it."

"Sounds . . . sounds clinical." She tried to laugh and failed. She dreaded his tale, yet didn't know why.

He pulled back from her, rubbing his nape, then stood and paced the room. "You've met my aunt and sister." At her nod he looked grim. "They've said I should've told you long ago. And I should have. At the time I thought it was better to let it be. I was wrong."

"Rafe, you don't—"

"I do, Cass." He looked away from her. "When I was growing up, my family life was strange. My parents lived a separate life from Linnie and me. I mean really apart. We saw them now and then, my father more often than my mother, but neither one that often. They had a fast-paced social life and were rarely home."

He glanced at her. "When we first met, I told you my parents started Brockman Associates with my uncle Edward, my father's brother, Aunt Adela's husband."

Cassie nodded. "Your real estate company and consulting firm."

"They were a terrific team. Uncle Edward was the CEO and oversaw the whole operation. My mother was a genius with people. They said she could persuade anyone to part with anything if she put her mind to it. My father had an eye for prime real estate. Whatever others saw as trash, he saw as an interesting makeover. My uncle gave them free rein in the business, but he somehow managed to keep their social life in check.

"My parents loved their work and did it well. I can understand that. I find the business a great challenge. And Linnie's like our mother. She has a talent for finding the right way to advertise our best side. But unlike our mother, Linnie could give up the business at the drop of a hat. Maybe I could, too, though I like it. But it isn't my life. And it sure isn't Linnie's."

Cassie knew he was leading up to something very heavy. She had to bite her lip to keep from screaming at him to be quiet, yet she wanted to know, was eager to have him open up to her.

"Anyway," he went on, "from the time Linnie and I were small, we knew we came second to the company, to our parents' social life. Neither parent was ever nasty or physically abusive. They just weren't there."

Neglect, Cassie thought. That cold, clinical backing away from involvement. She barely stemmed a shudder.

"In many ways it wasn't that bad. Linnie and I were very close. I took care of her and loved her. She depended on me and loved me. And there was always Aunt Adela. We spent a great deal of time with her and Uncle Edward. Things were pretty good, until he died." Rafe rubbed the back of his neck, squinting at the wall.

"If this is too rough—"

"It is, but it needs saying. And I'm going to tell you."

"All right."

"When Uncle Edward died of a heart attack five years before my parents' death, Linnie and I thought we'd lost our real father. And with his death, my parents' lifestyle became a frenetic marathon search for the elusive. I don't know what they were looking for, but it took them even further away from us. Aunt Adela tried talking with them, pleading with them, but they couldn't get off the wheel. Then that last Christmas . . ."

He paused, drawing in a deep breath. "Linnie was in boarding school at the time. I was in my first year of college. We were going to be together at Christmas for the first time since term began."

Cassie felt as though she were having a tooth extracted through the back of her skull. She didn't want to hear more, but she knew she must.

"On Christmas Eve I went out to do my shopping. Aunt Adela was coming to pick us up that afternoon and take us to her place for Christmas. My father was out somewhere too. Only my mother and Linnie were home, and Mother was . . . entertaining a new boyfriend. I didn't even think it might be unsafe to leave Linnie there. Aunt Adela was due to arrive any minute. I didn't realize a small twist of fate would turn our lives around." He shook his head. "She'd gotten caught in a Manhattan gridlock. When I got back, it was too late. The police were already there."

Cassie threaded her hands so tightly they ached.

"It seemed that my mother's new boyfriend was annoyed that she'd passed out after an overabundance of Christmas cheer and couldn't give him what he wanted. Delmar Givens was his name. He went upstairs, found Linnie, and raped her. She was fourteen years old at the time." At Cassie's choked gasp, he looked at her, a muscle jumping at the side of his mouth. "Forgive me, love. I know this is a shock."

Tears choked her throat. She nodded for him to continue.

"My father came home shortly after Linnie had been attacked. He went upstairs and figured out what had happened. I suppose he went mad. There was a struggle. They fought out of Linnie's room to the stairs. They fell down. Givens died of a broken neck." He paused and took deep breaths. "I assume Father woke my mother from her stupor and dragged her out to the car. I suppose he told her what happened. According to the police, they sped through Manhattan, heading upstate. I can only imagine what they said to each other on that damnable journey. On an icy stretch of road outside White Plains, they crashed. Both died."

Silence stretched between them.

"Linnie was catatonic for a long time. Fortunately she's had the best therapy, and she deals with it well most of the time." His smile was wry. "It would seem she did better than I. I didn't realize what a time bomb I was, what a coiled-up mess I was, until you left me. After I got over my drinking bout—my first and last flirtation with alcohol—I started looking at myself. And I didn't like the picture." He paused. "I'm sorry that I didn't go for counseling before we met. Things might've gone differently for us."

"We don't know that," she said, aching to comfort him.

He went to her and pulled her into his arms. "I won't be closed with you ever again, Cass." He kissed her gently on the lips. "I'll let you get dressed now." He looked down at her, enfolded in a voluminous bath sheet, and smiled crookedly. "You're beautiful."

She wanted to call him back even as the door was closing behind him, but she sensed he needed some time alone. It had been a revelation, not just what he'd told her, but that he could tell her at all. He had been so reserved, so private, when they'd first been together. Oh, he was more than affectionate and loving in his actions, but she'd always known there was a deep, hidden part of him. Now, he seemed determined to hide nothing. Cassie wasn't quite sure what to do with this man who was so different from the one she'd fallen in love with.

At a few minutes past seven Cassie stood poised on the last step above the foyer, listening for the sound of voices. She would have been on time, except that every few minutes as she was dressing, pieces of the story Rafe had told her echoed in her mind, and she had to stop as pain and sorrow swept through her. That he and his sister had suffered so. And knowing about his parents, how they'd treated him, explained so much of why Rafe had always held part of himself back from her.

It explained, too, why Rafe didn't drink. In an age when most men and women drank at least socially, she had wondered about Rafe's abstemiousness. She didn't drink herself, although everyone else in her family drank beer, wines, and liqueur on occasion. She'd overindulged when she was seventeen, and the prolonged stomach upheaval that followed was enough to make her vow never to drink again. Her brothers had told her it was a fluke, that she wouldn't do that every time. She listened to them but didn't drink. She saw no reason to court such a nasty condition.

"Waiting for something?" Rafe whispered at her side.

Startled, she swung to face him. "I was trying to figure out where you were."

"My aunt and sister are in the dining room."

She didn't answer but simply stared at him. He looked so elegant, she mused, in his dark suit, cut to flatter his broad shoulders and trim waist. As though her hand had a life of its own, it reached up and touched his cheek. Heat rushed through her, and she had to struggle not to step into his arms. "But you came out of the living room," she managed to say.

"Yes," he said hoarsely. "I was waiting. . . ." His voice trailed off, and he blinked, as though he was seeing her for the first time. "That outfit. The gown." He swallowed, his gaze coming back to her face. "You brought out the heavy guns tonight."

"Yes. I've decided that I'll use every weapon in my campaign." Where had those words come from? She'd been acting like a fool since they'd met at Rockefeller Center. But she couldn't call back the words, and she didn't want to.

"You have a campaign?" Rafe asked, lifting his hands to clasp her waist. Blood pounded through him at the feel of her. He'd spent the first months of their separation telling himself that he could get along without her. He'd spent the last two years knowing it would be impossible. He hadn't been able to manage much without her. Oh, he'd got ahead in business, but his personal life had been a desert. He hadn't wanted anyone but her. He moved closer, till their bodies were a bare inch apart. "Tell me about your campaign," he murmured.

"One should never reveal a military strategy," Cassie said. Why was her voice so breathless? And what was she talking about? She had no campaign. All she knew was that a solid confidence was building inside her. With every passing minute she was more sure she didn't want to lose Rafe. Was that what he wanted too?

Abruptly her confidence deserted her, and she felt as confused as she'd been when they'd lived together. She'd been all at sea, frustrated, trying to figure out what was wrong. Would it really be different this time?

Rafe saw the hurt and wariness on her face. Was she thinking of their painful past? Damn! If he'd been more open with her . . .

He caught her close to him, lifting her off the step and molding her body to his. "I, too, have a plan," he whispered. He nibbled at her mouth, and when she sighed and slipped her arms around his neck, he parted her lips, and his tongue touched hers in all the remembered ways. He wanted her for all time. And he wanted to undo the past, rewrite it, keep her as he wanted to be kept by her.

Cassie pulled back. "That was quite a welcoming kiss." She tried to smile, but she was shaking so much inside she couldn't.

"It was a Merry Christmas kiss," Rafe said huskily. He moved closer again and trailed kisses down her cheek. "Come with me for a moment."

She glanced toward the dining room. "Won't your aunt and sister be waiting?"

"They'll be fine. Jeeves has set out some canapés. He's eating with us, by the way."

"Oh. Perhaps I should help him."

"No need. He has first-class help if he needs it. Aunt Adela and Linnie are capable."

"Your aunt," Cassie said incredulously, "helping Buster?" Picturing that made her want to laugh. His aunt might be adorable, but she'd be chaos personified in a kitchen. And Buster Dunn was persnickety about his kitchen.

Rafe saw her lips quiver. "Yes, you're right. Aunt Adela might drive Jeeves crazy. But he can handle it. It's Christmas Eve."

"Yes." She looked away. "A very special day."

He took her arm and led her into the living room. "What's wrong?"

"Nothing. It's just that what you told me about your family is very fresh in my mind."

"It's not easily forgotten." His smile was twisted. "Linnie did better than I."

"You're her brother. Mine would've been frantic. I can understand that pain."

"Thank you, Cass. I just wish I'd told you sooner."

"We can't go back," she whispered.

"But we can go forward." His smile widened. "I'm happy you're here."

"I am too." Even more than she was able to tell him. She looked around the spacious living room. "I always liked this room. Your renovations make it even warmer, more homey."

He led her to the couch by the fireplace. "I was hoping you'd like the changes." He sat close to her, her hands in his. "I've a great deal to tell you about my life, about my family, and I intend to do it. Not all this evening, though. I was hoping you could stay in New York longer. I know you don't need to go back to Valdez until New Year's."

Cassie nodded, her heart thudding against her breastbone at his hot look. "If I can change my plane reservation. Rafe, shouldn't we go—"

"Not yet." He removed a small jewel case from his pocket. "Merry Christmas, darling." He opened the case and pushed it into her hands.

She stared down at the case, staying his hands when he would've removed the ring from it. "I've never seen anything so lovely." A large rectangular emerald in a classic gold setting lay there on the velvet. "You shouldn't . . ." Her voice trailed off. "I love it. I want to wear it." And she did, with all her heart. She smothered the voices deep inside that warned her of yesterday's pain. She wanted Rafe, she wanted to wear his ring. Surely there was a way to surmount their problems, to settle their differences. Hadn't he been open with her that very evening?

Yes, a voice argued, but can you trust him with your heart?

Yes, yes, she answered, praying she wasn't wrong.

He removed the ring from the case and lifted her left hand. When she pulled back and gave him her right, he hesitated, then nodded. He slipped the ring on her third finger, and its light flashed against her skin and the pale orange of her dress. "You're exquisite, Cassie. And I've missed you, badly." He caught her in his arms, pressing his mouth to hers.

Cassie's heart pounded up into her throat, her desire for this man more overpowering than anything she'd ever felt. "Rafe, Rafe," she whispered against his mouth.

"Cassie, I want you to come back to me. It's not too early to ask you to marry me, even though I swore I wouldn't propose to you right away. That I'd give you time." He inhaled an unsteady breath. "But I don't want to wait."

"Rafe." She wanted him, too, but there was so much still between them.

"Tell me I'm not going too fast. Cosmo told me to hang back."

"Cosmo? You talked to him about this?" Confusion and wonder rose in her.

"I talked to him two and three times a week. Either he called me or I called him." He smiled sheepishly. "I couldn't go for too long not knowing how you were doing. We parted under less than great circumstances. . . . Never mind that. We'll talk about it another time. Tell me you'll come back to me."

She wanted to, but she didn't. "Not yet, Rafe. I have to go back to Valdez, talk to my family—"

He silenced her by pulling her into his arms and kissing her again. The urgency in his touch fanned her desire to a near conflagration. Though her mind and heart counseled her to go slowly, her body was desperate to meld with his once more.

"I want you," he said roughly, his hand running over her, his desire evident in every taut line of his body.

"And I want you." She inhaled shakily. "But we wanted each other before, Rafe. And we had problems."

He nodded, sighing. "I know, darling."

She touched his face. "There's so much I don't know about you."

"I want to tell you all. Do you believe me?"

"I think you believe you want to tell me everything. But you've been a secretive man for a long time."

"Yes. But I want to be open with you, just as I want to know everything about you."

Cassie hesitated, feeling she was on a slippery precipice. "I want that. But I've come to believe that sometimes that's not possible. You'll have to understand that I have a hidden section of myself, too, that belongs just to me."

Her words obviously shocked him. "You've changed."

"I've grown."

"I can accept that, and that we have our work cut out for us to make our relationship lasting and solid. But I think we're worth the effort. Do you?"

Feeling teary, afraid but elated, she nodded.

He kissed her again. "We'll have each other for a lifetime, just the two of us."

She drew back, not willing to commit herself fully yet. "Just the two of us?" she repeated. "No children?"

He frowned. "I want to think about us, not about any . . . others in our life."

An alarm bell clanged in her head. "I do have a family. So do you."

"Oh, I know, I know. I don't mean them—"

"Are you two going to stay in here all evening? We should eat." Linnie stood at the wide entrance to the living room, looking pained. "I'm hungry."

"You're always hungry." But Rafe smiled and took Cassie's hand, lifting her to her feet. "You've met my sister."

"Yes," Cassie said.

"We've had a talk," Linnie said, arching a brow.

Rafe's sister was so much like him, Cassie thought. Strong and resolute, but with a vulnerability that spoke of remembered hurt. "Thank you for letting me share your Christmas," she said to the other woman.

"I'm glad you're here. You've been missed." She grinned at her brother, then turned and left the room. Her voice floated back to them: "Hurry up."

"She's quite lovely," Cassie said.

Rafe nodded as they walked down the short hall to the dining room. "Fragile steel."

Cassie looked up at him. "She's a lot like you."

"Thanks." He kissed the top of her head, then led her into the dining room. The candlelit room was festooned with wreaths and baskets of cones. Fir and pine boughs crossed and drooped from the shelf trim near the ceiling. Each corner had a miniature tree, dotted with orange and gold bows. It was a Christmas dream. Cassie looked around, delighted.

"Isn't it pretty, my dear?" Aunt Adela said.

"Very."

"I've never seen this place look so happy," Linnie said.

"Merry Christmas, ladies!" Rafe said, and helped Cassie to her chair on his right.

Buster bustled into the room, glowering at the table and those seated. "Is this a political rally? My food's getting cold."

"Jeeves is like me," Aunt Adela said. "He likes his food served hot."

Cassie laughed, then apologized when Adela looked at her inquiringly. "I don't call him Jeeves. He made that up. I use his real name, Buster Dunn."

Aunt Adela pondered that, then nodded. "I don't suppose it matters. I like all his names. Shall I call you Buster?"

"The little missus"—Buster jerked his head toward Cassie—"calls me Buster Dunn. I've gotten used to it." He swept back to the kitchen. "First course coming up."

He served the first course—French onion soup with a thick layer of melting cheese and fragrant croutons—with a flourish. With it were homemade rolls and crackers.

"Buster Dunn, you've outdone yourself," Linnie said, then laughed. "I've always wanted to say that."

"Please yourself, ya silly gal," Buster said affectionately, taking his chair after everyone was served.

"She will," Rafe said, laughing.

Cassie's heart pounded. He sounded so relaxed, so at ease. Watching him chat with the others and eat his soup with obvious enjoyment, she realized she was seeing the side of him she'd searched for in vain three years ago.

He caught her speculative look. Frowning, he grasped her hand and lifted it to his mouth. "I treated you shamefully, didn't I?"

She shook her head. "No, no. You always treated me well. You just wouldn't let me in. . . ."

He turned her hand over and kissed the palm. "Never again." He smiled into her eyes. "It hurts me to talk about my parents and Linnie, but I've come to realize I blamed myself for what happened. I know now it wasn't my fault."

She squeezed his hand. "Of course it wasn't. I'm sorry you suffered. I wish I'd known, I could have helped."

He leaned toward her. "You did help."

Just before his lips touched hers, they became aware of the silence in the room. Both straightened abruptly, and Cassie smiled wanly.

"Soup's delicious," she said.

"Would be if ya'd try it," Buster said.

When the dessert of flaming pudding and cookies was eaten, Aunt Adela rose to her feet. "Come along, Buster. Linnie and I will help you in the kitchen."

Buster stared at her in alarm. "There's no need, miss—"

"We've enough time before we have to leave for Saint Patrick's. And we want to, don't we, Linnie?"

"Sure. All in the Christmas spirit, Buster."

"Heaven protect me," muttered the recipient of their holiday giving.

The cathedral was packed, and the service was long, involved, and filled with the seasonal music. Throngs of persons bumped hips, shared missalettes, sang out strongly. There could be joy for this one night, as strangers were bonded by the hope of the season.

After the final hymn and the choir's "Hallelujah Chorus," Cassie asked the Brockmans to wait while she went to light a candle at the Little Flower's shrine. When she was out of earshot, Rafe leaned toward his sister and aunt. "How would you like to spend New Year's Eve in Alaska?"

Aunt Adela looked startled. She thought about it for a moment, then nodded. "I think I'd like that."

Linnie nodded too. "Did Cassie suggest that?"

"No," Rafe said. "I'm going to suggest it to her."

Linnie and Aunt Adela exchanged glances, obviously surprised by his unusual casual and carefree attitude.

"What if they throw us out the door?" Linnie asked. "I understand it can get cold there."

"Not to worry, dear," Adela said. "We'll wear thermal underwear." She leaned toward her nephew as she watched Cassie make her slow way back to them. "You've waited a long time for her."

He nodded. "There were many times when I thought it could never be. I want to care for her, nurture her all her days."

"Your uncle Edward would be proud."

Rafe smiled and patted her hand.

Cassie arrived back at their pew, and Rafe took her arm as they headed toward the exit, barely noticing the chattering throng around them. "Would you mind if I accompanied you back to Valdez?"

Flushed with pleasure, Cassie shook her head.

"I'd like your sister and aunt to meet my family too."

"Good, because I invited them to join us."

"You did?" She stared at him, mouth agape.

"Yes. Too bold?"

"No. No, I like it."

"Good." He kissed her nose.

Aunt Adela turned. "Will we stay in your house in Valdez, Rafe?" She bit her lip. "Oh, dear. Have I been indiscreet?"

Rafe's smile was tinged with loving exasperation. "I did want to surprise her, but it's all right, Aunt Adela." His smile widened when Cassie looked suspiciously at him.

What house? The words hung in the air, unspoken but strong.

"I bought a house in Valdez," he explained, "back in the summer. Cosmo knew about it. He helped me, along with your brother Lars. It's called the Bigelow House."

Cassie gaped at him. "The Bigelow House? That lovely old place on the hill? You bought that?" Without even knowing it, I still loved you, she wanted to add, but didn't. She was beginning to think Cosmo must have had the same conversations about love with Rafe as he'd had with her. "You have to trust love completely," he'd said once. "Be willing to risk everything for it." Apparently Rafe had taken that piece of advice to heart.

She was aware of him watching her closely as she got into the limousine he'd rented and settled beside Adela. She felt dazzled, confused, unable to think clearly.

"I wanted to make you happy," he whispered in her ear.

"Everything is going so fast."

"We'll talk later." He put his arm around her.

The drive through the Manhattan night was magical. Despite the traffic there was a hush, a brilliance that transcended the neon and concrete. The city had bowed to the season. The streets looked like flat licorice, the buildings had a candy-cane sheen, and the sky glittered like a cloth of diamonds above them.

Cassie was so bemused by everything, she scarcely realized they were out of the vehicle and in the apartment until she looked around her.

"We're off to bed," Aunt Adela said brightly. "Merry Christmas, Rafe, Cassie. It's been a wonderful evening." She kissed each one, then put her arm around Linnie.

Cassie watched them go up the stairs.

Rafe touched her arm, and she followed him into the living room.

She eyed him feeling shy, confused. "You're staring."

"Yes. I guess I can't get enough of looking at you," he said, then laughed at her surprise. "I like saying what I think."

"Then you'll get along with my brothers," she said dryly. "They do it all the time."

Rafe moved toward her, stopping just inches from her. "I want to make love to you, right on this floor."

The world wheeled. She couldn't get her breath. "Sounds informal." What a time to be squeaky-voiced, she thought. She sounded like a terrified mouse.

"Very." He took hold of her arms. "How do you feel?"

"Fine."

"I mean about making love on the rug."

"Oh. Well, I guess . . . I think . . . not bad."
She shook her head. "It's so strange being here
with you. Unreal."

His arms slipped around her waist, and he took
that extra step to make their bodies touch. "It's
very right that you're here with me. I found you on
Christmas Eve the first time."

She smiled. "That Christmas was unforgettable."

He chuckled. "I enjoyed that holiday meal."

"Because you watched us scarf the food. Meals
were not as regular for us."

He leaned down and kissed her cheek. "You ate
like a truck driver. And it was hardly a gourmet
dinner."

"To us it was."

For a moment they were in another time with
Raymond and Cosmo on Christmas Day, and they
were eating as if it were their last meal. The
memory burned in Cassie. Every time she'd
looked up from her sumptuous meal, Rafe had
been staring at her. She'd smile and he'd smile
back, but his eyes had held a hot, wanting look
that had seared her. She couldn't recall what was
said, only that she'd wanted to stay in the lovely
warm cocoon of Rafe's glance. He'd been Christmas happiness. She'd loved him so quickly, so
completely.

"I was jealous of Cosmo and Raymond that
day," Rafe said, leaning his forehead on hers.

Cassie pulled back. "You're kidding. Why?"

"Because I'd only known you for less than a day,
and they'd known you for months."

She chuckled, moving closer again, turning her head so that their lips met. They kissed long and slow, heads angling for comfort and enjoyment. It went on, deepening, pleasuring. Pulses raced, hands sought, bodies quivered in want. When Cassie pulled away, she was out of breath and trembling.

"So fast," she murmured. She stared at him. "What do you want, Rafe?"

"What I've always wanted. You."

He smiled down at her, his heart thudding. Could she see his excitement? He felt as though his blood had pumped clean through him. He loved her madly. It had been that way since meeting her. He'd been wise enough to know it hadn't happened that quickly with her. It had taken days, weeks, for her to fall in love. But by the time they'd moved in together, she'd been committed to him.

Despite that, he'd always had a suspicion that her love wasn't as total as his. That fear had never left him. He had it now. But love, an imperfect emotion in an imperfect world, was flawed itself, because it flowed through imperfections. He'd leave it at that, and never question her love for him.

Cassie felt his withdrawal, and her heart sank. Did he still have too many barriers? "Something's wrong. Will you tell me?"

He didn't answer, merely stared down at her. All her dreams started to shatter, and she stepped back from him, turning to leave.

"No." He grabbed her and pulled her back, holding her close, his mouth against her hair.

"Cassie. I've always loved you. I was just never sure you loved me as much."

Cassie felt frozen for a moment, shocked and angered. When she tried to wriggle free, Rafe wouldn't let her. "You knew that I loved you," she said, rearing her head back to glare at him.

"Yes."

"But you didn't think it was as much as you loved me?"

"Yes."

"Well, it was." She would've punched him if he hadn't had her hands pinned to her sides.

He smiled crookedly. "And you'd like to hit me for inferring anything else."

"Yes."

He hugged her. "Oh, Cassie, Cassie, I missed you."

"And I missed you."

"You sound like you missed me like a boil."

"At this point that's true."

"I wanted your love, Cassie. I was afraid I'd lose it."

Sharp words rose to her throat, but his pained, vulnerable look held them back. "Who didn't you believe in? Me or you?"

"Both, I suppose." He rested his forehead on hers. "It's important."

"I know. I'd like you to believe that I was very committed to you, or I'd never have agreed to live with you."

He sighed. "I know that. A big part of me knew that then, but I still had the sensation that I'd rushed you, coerced you. It made me unsure."

Even as his words angered her, she had the shaky sensation that Rafe was walking virgin ground, that he'd never made so many admissions before. Certainly he hadn't with her. She reached up and kissed him again, trying to put all her fears on the back burner.

"It's Christmas Day, and I have all I want," he said huskily. He lifted her right hand and kissed it. "Do you like your ring?"

"Very much."

"I look forward to seeing it on your other hand." He felt her tremble and tightened his arms around her. "I want that, Cass. I hope you do too."

"I want it to be right."

"We'll work on it."

They were silent for a few minutes, holding each other, reveling in the joy of being together again. Cassie was happy, happier than she'd ever been. And Cosmo, her good angel, was largely responsible. He'd always known she loved Rafe, and he'd kept in touch with him. Had he known, too, that meeting Rafe again would be so magical, almost as though they'd never parted? There'd been such a bond between them once, and it was strengthening again, despite the doubts. And why not? she asked herself. She'd never felt parted from Rafe, she'd felt bereft of his presence. But she didn't need to suffer that any longer . . . if she'd just trust in love and keep him.

She leaned back and smiled at Rafe. He had proved he wanted them to be together, not just with words but with a solid Christmas gesture. "I love the Bigelow house."

He blinked. "Where did that come from?"

"I was just thinking about it."

"I hope you'll like it enough to live in it."

"That could happen."

"I don't know what game you're playing, Cassiopeia Nordstrom, but I'm willing to participate."

"I didn't invite you in," she said, smiling.

"I'm in, lady." He kissed her cheek. "I would like my present now."

She stiffened. "I didn't get you one." Regret laced her voice.

He took her by the arm and led her to a brass music stand. A straight-backed chair sat before it, and on the chair was a long, narrow box wrapped in shiny gold paper. Cassie hesitated for only a moment, then tore off the paper, revealing a case. She thumbed the latches open and lifted the lid. Inside a silver flute gleamed in its nest of royal-blue velvet.

"Play for me," Rafe said softly.

Cassie reverently fitted the three pieces of the flute together. "It's a very good one."

"The best I could find." He went to the piano stool and sat down.

Cassie felt shy for a moment, but the instant she put the flute to her lips, her uncertainty vanished. Her world became music. Eyes closed, she played the sonatas and cantatas she'd been schooled in, notes that were as familiar to her as her skin.

The music soared and fell, then rose again in sweet, tremulous compliment to the season, to her family, to the loss of Cosmo . . . to the joy of finding Rafe.

Rafe was entranced. He'd often listened to her play when they'd lived together, but then she'd been rehearsing, practicing. Now, she seemed to have given herself over to her music, and it held her in delectable sway. The room itself seemed caught up in the sweet melodies. He didn't realize anyone was there, until his aunt touched his arm. Linnie was standing beside her.

"We heard it from upstairs," Adela whispered. "She's magnificent."

"Wonderful," Linnie said, patting her brother's shoulder.

"I think she might've been a virtuoso," Rafe said thoughtfully. For a moment he felt guilty. Not once had he asked her how it had felt to leave Juilliard. She'd given up a promising career to become a protector and a teacher. Had she regrets? His heart squeezed at the thought that she might have felt cheated. And he'd not been there to help her. Had he hindered her hopes? Guilt nagged at him. Had he wanted her attention too much?

The solo ended in an upcurve of sweet, strong notes that rode the air and settled slowly.

"Outstanding," Adela murmured, then she motioned to Linnie, and the two left quietly.

Rafe barely noticed their departure. He was caught in a strange web of guilt, acceptance, rejection.

Cassie rose and carefully replaced the flute in its case. Smiling, she turned to Rafe. Her smile faltered when she saw his stern expression as he walked over to her.

"What is it, Rafe?"

"You were magnificent," he said tightly. "You could've been a virtuoso."

Cassie frowned, not sure what he was saying. "Maybe," she replied.

"No! You would've been." He took hold of her upper arms. "I came into your life, swallowing you. Then Cosmo needed you—"

She put her hand over his mouth, shaking her head. "Wait a minute. I sacrificed nothing, Rafe. I wanted to move in with you. I still practiced and went to school. When Cosmo needed me, I was glad to take him to Valdez."

"But you've always regretted losing that time at Juilliard."

She was surprised. "No. I didn't at all. I knew what I wanted to do and I did it. Cosmo was important to me. And I never felt deprived when I lived with you." She swept her arm, indicating the room. "This was my music place, and you put many pieces of rehearsal equipment at my disposal, including that fine grand piano. No, Rafe, I won't let you think like that. The pain of leaving you"—she swallowed hard—"stayed with me. It had nothing to do with Juilliard. I was glad to be back with my family. I'd missed them." When he would've taken her in his arms, she moved back. "I—I think I'll go to bed now."

"Merry Christmas," he muttered, feeling a little lost. She'd left him so quickly.

Four

Cassie waited an hour. It probably wasn't long enough, since Adela and Linnie might not be asleep yet, but she was too impatient to tarry. She hadn't known until she was ready for bed and about to slide between the sheets that she wanted to spend the night with Rafe. She'd eyed the unoccupied bed and memories of nights spent with him washed over her. No, she was definitely not spending the night alone.

She put aside the book she'd been reading and donned the light traveling robe she'd brought from home. Not sexy, but it did keep the drafts away. Not that there were many drafts in Rafe's apartment. She grimaced at her reflection in the full length mirror. She really didn't look very sexy. She cocked her head and grinned. So? She felt it.

She opened her door and peered down the hall, first one way, then the other. All clear. Moving rapidly but quietly, she tiptoed along the corridor to the master suite.

At Rafe's door she took one more look around, then tried the knob. It turned silently, as well oiled and cared for as the rest of the place. The room was only semidark. Light came from the fireplace, where the low fire that Rafe preferred was burning steadily. The reading light above his bed was out. Was he asleep?

She could make out the mound on the bed she assumed was him. Was he nude? When they'd been together, he'd always slept in the buff. Excited and aroused just by being in the bedroom where she'd given herself time and again to the man she loved, she had to pause and take deep breaths.

Rafe must've heard. "Who is it? Jeeves?"

She moved quietly to the bedside, waiting for him to look up and see her. He didn't.

"Jeeves, whatever it is, tell me tomorrow," Rafe said tiredly, his head still buried beneath the covers.

Cassie took off her robe, eased back the covers, and slipped into bed. "Call him Buster," she said softly.

The covers were thrown off both of them as Rafe jackknifed up and around to a sitting position. He shook his head, as if he were trying to awaken from a lifelike dream. "Cassie."

"Yep. Now will you lie down? I'm getting cold."

He turned and rolled toward her at the same time, his hands reaching for her. "Cassie!"

"You keep saying my name." She lifted her own hands and pushed back his hair, cupped his cheeks, indulged in the tactile deliciousness of touching him.

"I can't believe you're here."

"Merry Christmas."

"And are you my gift?" He slipped his arms around her, easing her into the curve of his body. "You played for me. Now you're here. It is Christmas. My gift."

"Yes. And you're mine." She felt him quake as though he were chilled. "You're shaking as much as I am."

"Are you cold, darling?"

"Not now." She turned her face into his neck, her arms going around his waist. "I want you, Rafe."

"I want you, my only one, now and all my days. I have since the beginning, since that fateful Christmas Eve."

She chuckled, reaching up to pull his head down to hers. "I wasn't totally sure I hadn't run into the Manhattan ax murderer who happened to be a classy dresser."

"Well, at least you liked my clothes. On Christmas Day I think you were more interested in what I was feeding you."

"You were right about that. Cosmo, Raymond, and I lived on a great many peanut-butter-and-jelly sandwiches. The feast you set before us took precedence over everything." She ran her fingers over his chest, tugging at the crisp black hair there, feeling the sexual pull that his body always had for her. She leaned back, one hand fumbling for the light switch she knew was over her head.

Rafe grinned. "Changed?"

Cassie nodded as the light flared and they were spotlighted. He'd always been the one who had wanted the light on. She eyed him hungrily. "It's been a long time, Brockman. I want to see all of you. I missed you."

"And I missed you, lady."

He ran his fingers along her arm to her hand. "I'm feeling a great deal more Christmasy."

"Sounds good to me," she said huskily.

"I'd like to show you how much it means to have you here."

"Please do." Excitement all but choked her. She was here in his arms, the way she'd always wanted to be, the way she'd needed to be.

He gazed down at her. "Oh, Cass, I'm going to make you so happy."

"I'm happy now."

"Hang on. The intensity level just turned to overdrive."

She laughed, but her amusement fled, turning into passion, when his mouth scored down her ear to her neck, taking little bites and then soothing the bites with his tongue.

He slid down her body, his chest pressing against her breasts. She ached for him to kiss her there, but he turned his head to the side. She almost asked what he was doing, then she felt his tongue coursing down her arm to her hand. He nibbled on each finger.

"Having fun?" Her voice had a squeak to it again.

"Yes, I am. I hope you are."

She wanted to take part in the game, but the heat waves were beginning to overwhelm her. The contact of his hot skin against hers made her pant. All the remembered wonder of their days together washed over her like a tidal wave, whirl-

ing her into the madcap sexual vortex she'd
longed for for years.

His hands came up and caressed her breasts as
his mouth wandered over her body before joining
them. She cried out as he kissed and suckled.

The world had become a cauldron of throbbing
emotions, silencing the outside world, emptying it
of all but them.

Rafe lifted himself over her, bracing himself on
his elbows and rubbing his chest hair over her
breasts. "Oh, baby, I've wanted this for so long."

She tried to speak, but all that came out was a
guttural sigh.

He made a low groaning sound, then his mouth
came down on hers.

Carnal, hot, throbbing, she felt drowned in
sensations. Her body arched up to meet his,
wanting him, her passion telling the man she
loved that she desired him.

Groaning, Rafe released her mouth so he could
kiss her breast again. He massaged the soft orb as
his tongue teased her taut nipple. His libido shot
through the roof, his heart thudded out of rhythm.
He surrendered to the wonder of her, wanting the
joining more than he'd wanted anything in his life.

"You're killing me," he said, sighing happily.

"Wait till I get started," she said.

His hot laugh spurred her on, and she let her
hands explore him. At last she was living her
dreams, acting out those long, long nights of
imagining herself caressing Rafe. When she felt
that wonderful remembered hardness against the
junction of her body, she gasped with joy.

"You make me very hot," he said, kissing her
belly. "You could always do that."

"Wasn't very difficult."

He chuckled, rubbing his face between her breasts. Then he looked up at her. "Let's see how hot you are." Holding her gaze with his, he slowly slid his hand down her body to the apex of her thighs, nestling through the blond curls there to find her womanhood.

She cried out and pressed against his hand. He murmured approvingly at how hot she was, and his words were as exciting as his touch. Her legs began a rhythm of their own, rubbing up and down his as her body arched up toward his, begging for fulfillment.

Rafe leaned back from her, his breath ragged and uneven, his features taut and strained. "Wait, darling. It's been so long. It'll be over too soon if we don't take it easy."

"I thought we were," she said breathlessly, mirth rising with her passion. "I really like this. I wonder if any other man is as great a lover as you."

Happiness deluged him. Had she just told him there'd been no other? He had no right to ask her that, but the thought of it gave him great joy. "I hope you're not going to run a survey," he said, his chuckle rough, sensual.

"Not really." She sat up abruptly, letting her tongue rove his ear as she tamped down the sudden stab of disappointment. Why didn't he know there'd been no one but him? She pushed away the errant thought and caressed him again.

Rafe had noted her infinitesimal withdrawal and wanted to question her. He needed to know her uncertainties about him. Was she having second thoughts about being involved with him and his macabre family? No, he wouldn't think that way. He put it out of his mind and concentrated on the strong sensuous pull of his woman, held so close to him.

He let his tongue score a course between her breasts, his body shaking with want. In a tumult of emotion he possessed her with his tongue and hands, her gasps and tiny screams such a spur to his passion that he felt fulfilled already, yet wanting so much more.

"Rafe! I want you," she gasped.

"You have me. I'm here with you, darling."

The gentle joining became a cataclysmic clash of passions. Neither knew where a body began or ended. They were one as only lovers could be. Love took them, blew them apart, then knit them back together with care, cuddling them, keeping them.

She woke in the night. When she turned, Rafe was there, taking her quickly. Once more at dawn she murmured his name, and he was there, his leisurely lovemaking driving her mad, his mouth and hands testing her limits. Time and again he took her to the peak of the mountain, then backed off, keeping her from fulfillment, until she thought she'd lose her mind.

Trembling in ecstasy, she hauled him to her. "Make love to me, fool."

He laughed and did so.

"I could get used to this," she said when she had enough breath again to speak.

"That's the idea." He lifted his head to look at her. "Tell me honestly. Will you mind if I come to Valdez?"

She'd love it if he stayed there forever, but she

still wasn't ready to say that. "Not at all. After all, you do have a house there."

He eyed her sharply. "That's not a problem, is it?"

"You know it isn't."

His fingers traced over her hip. "I'd like my family to meet yours."

"Me too." She touched his face. "You continue to surprise me."

"Because I want commitment, because I want us?"

His openness was like a sweet balm to the pain her soul had suffered for so long. If she couldn't yet let down all of her barriers, she could feel many of them crumbling. "Yes," she whispered, reaching up to kiss him. "I like this new facet of the man."

"I want you to love all the man," he said, gently pushing her back down.

"I do," she whispered.

"Take me, my love."

And she did.

Christmas Day was a wild, joyous mountain of wrapping paper, laughter, food and drink, and lots of talk.

"I've never had such a full day," Adela said happily to Linnie.

Her niece patted her hand. "And there'll be more for all of us." She eyed her ecstatic brother, hovering over Cassie. "I truly feel that way now. They deserve their happiness."

Adela sighed. "They've certainly earned it."

• • •

The week between Christmas and New Year's flew by for Cassie. Rafe had to work at least a few hours each day, and she spent that time either with Adela or exploring Manhattan, rediscovering favorite haunts from three years before.

Regardless of what she did, though, she felt as if she were suspended in time, awaiting the moment when she would be with Rafe again. It had been like that three years before. Young and in love for the first time, she had plunged headfirst into the experience, exhilarated by the potent emotions he had roused in her. Now, however, she was more cautious. She knew those potent emotions could lead to pain as well as rapture.

So when she and Rafe were together, whether they were eating out or taking a walk through Central Park or just staying at his apartment, she made certain they talked. And Rafe obliged her. He told her more about himself, his childhood, his school years, his work, in those few days than she'd learned in months of living with him. What he revealed of himself—the lonely but determined boy he'd been and the remarkably successful yet often alone man he'd become—made her love him more each day.

And each night, when they closed his bedroom door and fell into each other's arms, she knew she could never leave him again. Yet still she could not say the words, could not break through that last barrier of wariness.

The day before they were to leave for Valdez, Rafe came home earlier than expected, his usual beaming smile missing when he greeted her.

"Trouble?" she asked.

"Maybe," he said. He led her into his study, closing the door behind them. When he turned to face her, his smile was wry. "You're going to think me a fool, Cass."

"Why?"

He took her hands. "I'm mad about you."

Relief swamped her. It couldn't be too important. "That's good to hear."

"Maybe too much in love with you." He kissed her forehead. "I've taken precautions every time we've made love . . . except that first night. Don't laugh. It isn't funny. I feel like a fool." He shook his head, frowning. "I was working on the Fryer contract this afternoon, and all at once it hit me. I can't believe I could be so careless."

"Why does it matter?" Cassie asked, truly baffled. She knew she hadn't definitely said she would marry him, but the issue really didn't seem to be much in doubt. Or was he still so uncertain about her love?

"It matters, Cassie," he said. His brow furrowed. "Is there a chance you could be pregnant? If there's even a suspicion, we should see an ob/gyn right away. Terminating a pregnancy isn't dangerous in the early—"

"What're you saying?" She pushed back from him, her hands closing into fists. "You can't make decisions like that about my body."

"Darling, listen to me. We have each other. We don't need children." He drew a deep breath, and when he spoke again his voice was harsh. "I have no intention of allowing my parents' bad seed to be promulgated."

She whirled away from him. "That's not just

your decision. If we marry, you'll condemn me to a childless life because of your arbitrary notions."

"They're not arbitrary, and I'm not saying you should be childless. We can adopt." He pushed his hand through his hair. "Take a look at the statistics. More aberrations of mankind can be laid at the feet of the gene pool than we've ever imagined."

"That's insane reasoning. No one in the world would have a child if they rationalized in such an absurd fashion." Voice rising angrily, she glared at him. "What makes you think you won't get a defective member of the 'gene pool' if you adopt?"

"Don't be foolish. Everything's a risk, I know that. But the risks with adopting are—"

"You can't make that decision alone."

"Don't be silly. I wouldn't do anything without consulting you."

"Wouldn't you?"

"Stop shouting."

"Then you keep your voice down. I've—"

The door was pushed open. Aunt Adela stood there. "Is something wrong? Linnie and I can't help but hear you."

"Sorry," Cassie mumbled. She crossed the room to the door, sidling around Adela.

"Cassie! Wait." When she ignored him and left, slamming the door behind her, he pounded his fist on his desk.

"Creating problems, Rafe?"

He swung around to face his aunt. "You know nothing of this."

"I know everything of this." She folded her arms in front of her. "Everything you do is colored by the past. You can't uncreate your creators, dear boy. It happened."

"I'm not trying to do that. I want the woman I love to understand my position."

"Just as you understand hers."

"You're being cute, Aunt."

"And you're grinding your teeth. Rafe, Rafe, for God's sake and for your future's sake, let go of the past."

"I'm trying to do exactly that. Excise my past. Cassie doesn't see that."

"Perhaps she sees a man unable to deal with it, a man who tries to act as though it didn't happen."

Rafe whitened. "I've dealt with my mother and father, and what was done to Linnie."

"But you've never dealt with what was done to you."

He stalked across the room. "I think I'll dine out this evening."

"Very well. Will you still be accompanying us to Valdez tomorrow?" Adela asked calmly.

"Of course."

"See you on the plane."

He paused at the door, looking back at his aunt. "You don't understand."

"Neither do you."

The plane flew west, the sun chasing it as it scampered over, through, and under scudding clouds. It would be a long flight, but first-class travel would make it bearable.

Cassie and Rafe talked politely to each other, smiled now and then, included Linnie and Adela in their conversation. Adela watched them with concern, while Linnie was in raptures, oohing and aahing over the plastic food, the clouds, the uniforms of the attendants.

"This is a girl who attended the Sorbonne," Adela told Cassie, smiling.

"You act like a fledgling flyer, Lin," Rafe said to his sister.

Linnie rounded on him. "Don't try putting a damper on things, Rafe. I can't be put down. I have a good feeling about this trip. It—it makes me happy."

Rafe reached across the aisle and touched her arm. "I'm glad." As he sat back, his glance slid to Cassie, sitting silent and pensive beside him.

Linnie chuckled. "And I'm glad for you. You're with Cassie again. And we finally got to meet her. I remember how Aunt Adela argued with you three years ago about wanting to meet her and how you held back, wanting to keep her all to yourself."

"Linnie," Adela said warningly.

Linnie ignored the warning. "You remember, Aunt. He'd visit us for five minutes, then he'd have to fly away to find Cassie wherever she was. And there was always some excuse why we couldn't meet her. I think Rafe was ashamed of us."

Catching the pained expression on Cassie's face, Linnie sat forward, alarmed. "What is it, Cass? Are you airsick?"

"No," Cassie managed to say. "Just the aftermath of Christmas, I guess."

"Yes," Adela said brightly. "I've noticed such a letdown too. Christmas was so wonderful this year. The best we've ever had, I think."

"Oh, it was good, wasn't it?" Linnie said. "Must be because you were with us, Cassie."

Cassie didn't answer but turned to stare out the window.

As Linnie and Adela began an intense conversation about the spring fashions in the *Vogue* magazine Linnie had brought along, Rafe took Cassie's hand and leaned close to her. "Don't you think we should talk about this?"

"Yes, I do," she said fervently, her voice as low as his.

"Cass, you know I don't want to hurt you—"

"You have hurt me."

He winced. "If you could just understand how I feel."

"If you could understand how *I* feel."

They had a short stopover in Seattle to change planes, then they were on their way again.

I'm going home, Cassie thought as the plane rose above the clouds. *With the man I love. Why do I feel such overwhelming sadness?* All the questions and none of the answers. She wanted to go to Rafe on her knees, beg him to take her, no matter what sort of problems they could suffer from their differences. A drop of love was better than a quart of nothing. A moment together was better than a lifetime alone. She turned to look at him, sitting across the aisle now with Linnie. The two of them had business to discuss. For a moment she resented his paying attention to anything but her, then told herself to be reasonable. She and Rafe certainly couldn't discuss their problems there. They needed privacy.

Facing forward again, she caught Adela's sympathetic look.

"Don't give up on him, dear," Adela said, squeezing her hand.

"I'll try not to," Cassie whispered back.

"You'll try not to what?" Rafe had turned at their words.

"Try not to throttle you."

His smile was fleeting. "That's comforting."

When they landed in Anchorage, a private jet was waiting to take them to Valdez. It was a quick flight, and as they circled the Valdez airport preparing to land, Linnie was fidgeting with excitement.

"I have this feeling," she said, "that I'm on the brink of something."

Cassie grinned. "It's Alaska. It gets to people."

As they taxied down the runway to the hangar reserved for private aircraft, Cassie could see a big man standing at the gate. "There's Kort. He's my youngest brother. Actually all my brothers are older than I am, but he's the youngest of the three."

"Where?" Linnie asked. "Oh. Whatta hunk." She pressed her face to the window. "Are they all that big and handsome in Alaska?"

Cassie chuckled. "Yes. And he's the shy one."

"Ummm. Sounds interesting."

Rafe and Adela exchanged happy smiles. Cassie could tell they were pleased at Linnie's breezy remarks. It didn't take a genius to figure that they worried about Linnie, even though the assault had taken place years ago and she seemed well adjusted. Rafe had told Cassie, though, that Linnie dated only rarely and had never been seriously involved with a man.

The jet finally reached the hangar and stopped. Cassie had to laugh as she saw her brother lift the gate attendant aside and stride onto the field. All three of her brothers had little patience with rules and regulations that seemed foolish to them.

"Here he comes, Linnie," she said.

"Isn't he beautiful?"

Cassie relaxed. She was home. "I've never thought of any of my brothers as beautiful."

Rafe turned to her, sensing the change in her. "You're glad to be home."

"Yes. This is real. Alaska is so real. The winters are beautiful." She turned to Linnie, who was watching the still-closed door expectantly. "You'll have to sharpen your skates, Linnie. We do a great deal of that."

"I can't skate."

Cassie smiled. "Not to worry. I'm sure one of my brothers will teach you."

The door opened at last, but before any of them could move, Kort stepped up into the plane.

"Kort!" Cassie waved.

"Hi, Sis." He smiled at her, then at Rafe and Adela. His smile fell when he looked at Linnie. He stared until she blushed.

"Kort," Cassie said, "you're holding up everyone."

Kort tore his gaze from Rafe's sister, eyed the rest of them, then leaned down and pulled Linnie to her feet. "Don't worry about your luggage. I'll take care of everything."

"I'm sure you will," Linnie murmured, craning her neck to look up at him.

"Young man," Adela said, trying to look stern, "are you going to make us stay here all day?"

Kort lifted his head, looking dazed and off balance. "Pardon me, ma'am. You must be Mrs. Brockman."

"I am. And that's my niece you have the death grip on. Shall we go?"

"Yes." Kort kept Linnie in front of him, rushing her off the plane.

"Where are his manners?" Cassie said in exasperated amusement.

"He has other things on his mind," Rafe drawled.

"Our mother would cuff him for his actions." Cassie shook her head, happy.

They deplaned and followed Kort and Linnie to the terminal.

"He isn't going to let her go," Cassie said, her amusement changing to bafflement.

"Of course not," Rafe said, not sounding at all concerned. "I'm surprised he's not carrying her."

"Don't be ridiculous," Cassie said. "Kort isn't a caveman."

"Sure he is. We all are when it comes to that special woman."

Five

The excitement of homecoming lasted all evening and far into the night. Since it was New Year's Eve, Cassie's mother, Mary, had decided to throw a small party to welcome the Brockmans. But the rumor had gone around town that Cassie was bringing home her fiancé, and chums of every sort, those close and those not so close, arrived at the Nordstroms' door throughout the night.

"Quite a family," Rafe said to Cassie a couple of hours into the celebration.

"Yes." She turned to smile at him.

"Pay no attention to my brothers," her sister Andy said, approaching Rafe. "They're Neanderthals, one and all."

Rafe grinned. "They talk like pretty smart ones."

Andy shrugged. "I guess they are." She looked across the room at her three brothers. "Willie, the middle one, builds boats. He built Daddy's fleet of three. He likes doing things with his hands."

Cassie laughed. "And he can even bake bread when the mood hits him."

Her sister Astrid joined them. "And Lars is in the fishing business with Daddy. Kort is their accountant." She eyed her brothers. "Even if they look like scaled-down Sumo wrestlers, they do have minds."

"Small ones," Andy said.

"I heard that," Mary Nordstrom said. "Stop picking on your brothers."

"Why? They're the bane of our lives," Andy said, and grinned when her mother frowned and said, "Girls."

"Mother, you didn't have as many guests at my graduation," Cassie said as she waved to yet another group of people.

"At all our graduations rolled up into one she didn't have this many," Astrid said, shaking her head.

"She wants to impress Adela," Andy said.

Mary bit her lip, her glance sliding toward Cassie. "I should be ashamed of myself, but she's such an elegant woman."

Cassie's mouth dropped open. She'd never seen her mother so nervous. "Mother, Adela's comfortable with any situation. And she's so unaffected. I admit I was afraid to meet Rafe's family, quite sure they'd look down on me, but—"

"Bull," Rafe said inelegantly, slipping an arm around her waist. "You'd face down King Kong." He smiled at Mary. "I like the party, Mrs. Nordstrom. Thank you for making us feel so welcome."

"Why don't you call me Mary, Rafe."

"Actually, unless you'd mind, I'd like to call you Mother."

Silence.

Conversations eddied around them, but the four women with Rafe didn't notice. They were stunned, mouths agape, staring at him.

"Did I say something wrong?" Rafe gazed from Cassie to her sisters to their mother. "Would that bother you, ma'am?"

"Bother me?" Mary said softly. "No, not at all. But . . ."

"I meant," he added, "as soon as the vows are said and we're husband and wife. Would that be all right?" He put his arm around Cassie. "I think the wedding will be soon."

"Do let me know when you decide," Cassie said acidly.

"I will." He kissed her nose and ambled away.

"Wow, he's something," Andy said. "Does he have a twin?"

"Don't be ridiculous," Cassie said. "Would you want another Rafe on this earth?"

"Don't be nuts, Cass," Astrid said. "Any woman would be glad to have him. If you weren't my sister, I'd make a run at him myself."

Cassie frowned at her sisters. An unpleasant leadish taste filled her mouth; the taste of jealousy. Her older sisters had always been her best friends, but at that moment she could hate them. Appalling!

"What's eating you, Cass?" her brother Willie asked, striding up to her. He easily picked her up so her feet dangled several inches above the floor. "You look great. I'm glad you're back."

"Me too." She grinned at her brother. "Now put me down, oaf." She was laughing, then she happened to glance sideways and see Rafe start toward her, his face grim. He stopped abruptly, eyeing her and her brother. It shook her to see his anger, fading now, but no less real. In all the time they'd lived together, she'd never seen Rafe out of control. It hadn't been that way a moment ago, and it was disconcerting.

Willie put her down, kissing her cheek. "I like your man. And he tells me you'll be marrying soon."

"He told me the same thing."

Willie laughed, but Cassie scarcely noticed. She was watching Rafe again. He was coming back.

"Think he'll punch me in the nose?" Willie whispered to her.

"Certainly not." She pushed her big brother away, then smiled at Rafe. "Pay no attention to my brother."

"Thank you," Willie said dryly.

Cassie glared at her brother. "They're always funning."

"I see," Rafe said easily. "Can I talk to you, Cassie?" Despite his polite tone, he gripped her arm firmly. "In private?"

Now what? Cassie wondered, sending a weak smile her brother's way. Willie's expression was a mixture of curiosity and concern. "How about the kitchen?" she suggested.

Rafe nodded, and they wended their way through the crowds of people to the kitchen. Surprisingly that room was empty, and Cassie closed the door behind them with a sigh of relief.

"Rafe—" she began, but he cut her off.

"Let's get married on Saturday," he said.

Cassie reeled. "We—we can't," she stammered.

I'm not ready, she said silently, but aloud said, "Too many steps."

"I think I can cut through the red tape. All I need is your response."

She stared at him for a long moment, realizing she had to make her decision now. She couldn't hide behind her fears any longer. "Will we be enough for each other?" she asked softly.

"You're more than enough for me."

"I don't mean for always. I mean do we have enough flexibility to understand each other, to give as much as we should, to receive gracefully?" She grimaced at her clumsiness in trying to express herself.

"Yes. I'm willing to make any accommodation, work things out. I didn't like my life without you."

She sighed. "I didn't like it much, either."

"Then take a chance."

"A long shot, you mean."

"Not so long." He ran his hands up her arms. "Say yes."

"I wonder what my parents would think," she said, her heartbeat quickening at even his light caress. "I don't think they'd figured on anything so soon."

"That's not an answer, Cass."

She gazed at him, remembering what it had been like without him. "Yes," she said.

Rafe was jolted to his shoes. "What?"

"You heard me."

"I'll hold you to it," he said hoarsely.

"Fine."

He whirled her around and kissed her, his mouth slanting over hers, his heart thudding against his breastbone, passion pulsing all through him. "I want you."

"I want you."

Neither heard the door open behind them, but they did hear Mary say, "We still have guests."

Rafe lifted his head, his eyes glazed. Mary, Helborg, and Willie stood clustered in the doorway. "Sorry, ma'am, my fault. I just talked your daughter into marrying me very soon."

"Good thing," Willie said before his parents could respond. He shoved his hand out to Rafe.

Mary cried and hugged her daughter.

Helborg cleared his throat over and over again, nodding fiercely, then hugging Cassie. "We will announce it to our friends."

"Fine, sir," Rafe said. "Saturday is the big day."

"That's in six days," Mary said faintly.

Rafe touched her hand. "I'll get all the help you need, ma'am."

"The church women will help too," Helborg said, patting her shoulder.

"They'll need to be told today," Mary said, plans already spinning through her mind.

"Don't fret," Rafe said. "Everything will be fine. I'll have a crew of workmen in here to do your bidding. I want you to relax."

Mary looked skeptical. "Relax about my daughter's wedding?"

"Absolutely."

Rafe said it with such assurance that Cassie had to smile. That part of him hadn't changed. He still thought it was only a matter of forethought and good planning to move mountains. He never saw the need to back down from any challenge.

"We'll all help, Mama," Astrid said, catching the gist of the conversation and kissing her sister's cheek. "It will be fine." She kissed Rafe's cheek too. "Got a friend like you? Or a twin maybe?"

He grinned. "Definitely a friend, and he'll come to the wedding."

"Things are looking up," Astrid said saucily.

A few minutes later they all moved into the capacious sitting room. A few curious glances were cast their way, but it seemed that most of the guests hadn't missed them. After all the smorgasbord was still laden with dainties and there were beverages aplenty.

Helborg called for attention. "Before my wife puts out more food, I have an announcement to make. My daughter Cassiopeia will be married this coming Saturday. Of course you are all invited. In fact, I would like you to tell my wife before you depart this evening if you'll be able to make the nuptials." His last words were all but drowned out as the guests surged toward Cassie and Rafe. "And how do you know who her groom is to be?" Helborg called loudly. "I haven't said his name."

Laughter was his only answer.

Cassie felt as though she were being packed into a can. All of their exuberant guests crowded forward for a kiss, for a congratulatory handshake, for a few words of wisdom.

"Cass," Thom Bedmill, a childhood friend, exclaimed, "I'm glad you're bound up. Lars might've made me make an offer, and I haven't the stamina to take on a Nordstrom."

Everyone laughed—except Rafe.

Cassie was used to Thom Bedmill. He'd been in and out of their house for years, just as all the

Bedmills had. She felt Rafe stiffen beside her, though, and quickly turned to him, putting a hand on his arm. "Don't be angry," she whispered. "That's Little Thom's way. He always speaks out of turn. Lordy, you aren't going to try and battle Little Thom, are you? He'll throw you clear across the sound."

"He isn't going to get away with talking to you that way," Rafe said mulishly, moving around her.

"Lars!" Cassie called frantically, throwing herself against Rafe's chest.

He tried to pry her away from him, but she clung like a barnacle. "Let go," he muttered.

"No."

He stared down at her. "No?"

"That's right. You're not getting into a brouhaha with the Bedmills. They're our neighbors, and we like them. Little Thom always puts his foot in his mouth. Everyone expects it."

Rafe's mouth tightened. "Not to you."

"Rafel, I expect you to behave," Adela said firmly. "You've been so busy protecting your women, me and Linnie, and now Cassie, that you forget we can take some good-natured ribbing and give back as good as we get. If Cassie feels the need to punch Little Thom, she'll do it."

"That's the ticket," Willie said, chortling. "Knock it off, Little Thom. My brother-in-law to be is very particular about what's said to his women."

Little Thom looked puzzled for a moment. He glanced at Lars, Kort, and Willie, then at Rafe. "No jokes, right?" he said.

Rafe's anger ebbed away as Little Thom held his hand out to him. The two men shook hands, and

Rafe realized how foolish he'd looked. Smiling ruefully, he lifted Cassie's arms from around his neck and fixed them to his waist. "I'll try harder."

Little Thom's laugh boomed over the assemblage. "So will I."

"Good enough," Helborg said. "Now, we'll talk about the wedding."

The women converged on Mary. The men headed for the drinks so they could toast the happy couple.

Helborg glanced at Cassie. "Can you handle him, do you think? Or should I get a platoon of marines?"

"She can handle me, sir," Rafe answered for her, and hugged her tight.

The next days ran together, merged into one chaotic merry-go-round.

Rafe enjoyed it, amazing Cassie with his never-ending smile, goodwill, and endless lines of helpers and workmen who'd converged on Valdez.

"It's amazing," Mary confided to Adela. "Just when I'm thinking about a chore that must be done, a gaggle of workers shows up and does it."

"My nephew is making quite sure nothing stands in the way of his wedding."

"I approve," his future mother-in-law said.

The wedding day was like a picture postcard.

Snow fell gently from the charcoal-gray sky, softening the stark lines of the bare tree branches, coating everything with a comforting blanket of white.

The bride wore cream, a satin gown with a fitted bodice and full skirt. She looked radiant and joyous. The groom wore a black silk suit with a white shirt, narrow pleates running down the front. He looked distinguished and in command.

The priest was bemused, all but overwhelmed at how fast the wedding had taken shape in his small church by the sound. He was not a stickler for the banns, but he'd been taken aback by the black-haired gentleman who didn't understand barriers, and therefore ignored them. Still, he'd seen how happy Cassie was and he felt in his heart that Rafe loved her. That was enough.

The exchange of vows wasn't long, but Cassie felt every word in her heart. When Rafe gave her her first kiss as his wife, she knew she'd done the right thing. Smiling happily at her husband, she silently thanked Cosmo.

In a whirl of activity they were whisked from the church to the large fireman's hall for the reception. The receiving line seemed to take forever, there were so many guests.

After Rafe had met his fiftieth student, he turned to his wife, puzzled. "How many do you teach?"

"About a hundred, but not on the same levels, and some of those are carryovers into the orchestra."

He stared at her. "Why don't you ever tell me about all your admirable qualities, your stamina, your commitment? A hundred students? That's fantastic."

"Do you tell me everything?" she asked.

He was startled by the unexpected question. "You know all about me," he said carefully.

"No, I don't." Though she regretted her ill-timed question, Cassie couldn't take it back. She grasped his hand, and his fingers curled around hers. "I don't think you've told me everything about your family. I want to know it all, Rafe." Including, she added silently, why he didn't want children. Because she very much wanted Rafe's children.

Moments passed, then he looked at her again. "I've told you everything, Cass. I've been open with you."

"Yes. But you still have hurts, Rafe. Maybe you don't even know they're there."

He stared at her. He seemed about to speak again, when a jovial voice forestalled him.

"Hey, lovebirds, the dancing is about to begin. You should start it."

Cassie glared at her brother Lars. She could've throttled him for interrupting them. "Guess we have to," she said instead.

Rafe nodded, his brow still furrowed. "I want to dance with you, darling."

Lars stared at her, puzzled by her flat tone. "Tummy upset, Cass?"

"You could say that," she muttered.

She and Rafe walked to the edge of the enormous oak-plank floor, which gleamed with coats of polyurethane. It was coated now, too, with powdered wax to make it easy to glide and step.

Rafe eyed the dance floor dubiously. "It's like snow. They might have gone overboard on the powdered wax."

"Uh-uh. You haven't done our dancing yet," Cassie said. "I was hoping we could put this off, but I suppose there's no time like the present to show you the wild side."

He turned his dubious gaze on her, then glanced at the expectant guests ringing the dance floor. "Something aerobic?"

"Never could fool you." She laughed as the first strains of a fiddle and harmonica split the air. "Here we go."

She was quite sure Rafe would never pick it up. The dances common to their friends and their families were a combination of Scottish, Norwegian, and Swedish country dances, with a little Texas two-step thrown in. Cassie had always loved the energetic dancing, but she had the feeling Rafe would hate it.

Rafe stumbled as he tried to follow Cassie down the room, whirling, bending, doing a skipping step that was both familiar and unfamiliar.

He'd have to be a fool not to realize that she hoped to keep him off balance, and he decided not to give her as much cause for amusement as she seemed to expect.

It was a travesty at first, but Rafe kept going, gritting his teeth, trying to master the groupings of swings, skips, turns, and bends. When he saw Cassie wave away her family when they would have joined them on the floor, he cursed under his breath. Damn her! She wanted him to make a fool of himself.

Bearing down, he concentrated on what they were doing.

"Damn, Brockman," she said breathily after a couple of minutes. "I think you've got it." She laughed.

"Yeah, Brockman, I think I have."

It was Cassie's turn to stumble at the use of her married name. She hadn't yet decided whether to keep her own name or take Rafe's. That decided her.

He grasped her around the waist and whirled her down the room as fast as he could. When her feet left the ground, he spun her without losing step.

Howling like banshees, her brothers joined them, refusing to be held back by their parents any longer. Kort grabbed a laughing Linnie and swung her around as though she weighed no more than a puff of snow.

Lars reached for Adela, who shook her head in protest. "Don't worry, ma'am," he said. "I'll go easy."

Willie took hold of Astrid, who warned him not to break anything. Helborg clutched his wife, laughing. Andy latched on to one of the Bedmills, and the music and the stamping of feet created a chaotic thunder that reverberated through the building and to the out-of-doors.

In moments the floor was filled, and the energetic dancers combed up and down and around the room.

Cassie tried to stop Rafe. Impossible. "You've got the bit in your teeth," she said, panting.

"This is great." He laughed and spun, when Willie caromed into him, keeping Cassie protected from the blow.

"Stop them," Astrid cried, pummeling her brother to no avail.

"No chance," Rafe said. He grinned at his new brother-in-law, who swung Astrid alongside Cassie. "This is great."

"I know," Willie said, and ducked when his sister swung at him.

Adela sank into a chair next to Mary while Lars and Helborg went to get them drinks. "I've . . . never . . . been so stimulated." She patted at her face, laughing.

"You're being kind," Mary said. "Lars is too strong for his own good. I noticed your feet rarely touched the ground."

Adela laughed. "It does prevent fatigue. Ahhh, lemonade." She accepted the glass from Lars and drank thirstily. "Very good."

"Yes." Mary frowned at her son's glass. "Did you put anything in the lemonade?"

"Mother, you told us not to."

"Did you?"

Lars shifted his shoulders. "Only in the punch bowl near—"

"Where all your friends are standing," Mary said.

"Yes."

Adela laughed again. "I might try some of that later."

"I would advise you to leave it alone," Mary said. "I'm not really sure what they would've put in it. My friend Freda Wierdan insists that the infernal brew her husband Matthias drank at his son's wedding is what made him bald."

"I like it here in Alaska," Adela said. "You know, I think I might stay. After all, Rafe will be here, and if I don't miss my guess"—she winked at Mary—"Linnie may be staying too.

"Since my husband's death, I only stayed in Manhattan for Rafe and Linnie's sake. But I really think Alaska is more my style than New York City.

And who knows, maybe the magnificent scenery around here will inspire me to be a better painter."

Mary smiled. "We would love it if you stayed. And I'm sure Helborg could help you to find a nice house to buy."

Adela nodded, her mind made up. "Yes, I think Alaska will be good for us all, Mary. Now and then you and I can fly to New York to shop or see a show."

"Just to shop?" Mary said faintly. "We can do that in Anchorage."

"Oh, well, we won't go all the time. Just once a season would be good. I'll keep my apartment, of course, so it should work. It won't be any expense at all."

"It won't?"

"Not one bit."

Finally Cassie was able to get Rafe off the floor and to a table near her mother and Adela.

"Dear," her mother said, frowning, "you look so frazzled. Brides should look serenely lovely. Shouldn't they, Adela?"

"Not when they're married to Rafe."

Cassie smiled at Adela, pushing back the damp tendrils of hair from her forehead. "I think I'll need combat training."

"Not if you stay in my bed," Rafe whispered.

"Even more."

Rafe laughed, then turned to watch the dancers, her hand caught in his.

Cassie studied him. He was a beautiful man, and she loved him. He'd melded with her family and joined in their exuberance as though he'd always lived such a life. He was a straightforward man in some ways, yet so complex in others. She'd married a paradox.

The party went on for hours. No one flagged. The musicians were sweaty and red-faced, but they showed no sign of stopping.

Finally Cassie turned to her new husband. "I think we can leave now." She smiled lopsidedly. "Not that I know where we're going."

He kissed her. "To our home, of course. I thought you'd prefer that."

"Our home," she said softly.

"Yes."

"You're right. I would like that."

The good-byes took forever. There was no easy way to get away from the guests, who kept talking to them, teasing them. Finally everyone backed away so Cassie could say good-bye to her family.

"Be happy, dearest," her mother said, touching her cheek.

Helborg stood behind Mary, nodding and smiling at his daughter.

"I will, Mom," Cassie said, clasping first one parent, then the other, then hugging her siblings.

Rafe kissed Mary's cheek, then Adela's and Linnie's, then he swept Cassie up into his arms. "Wave, Cass."

Cassie waved. The laughter of her family and friends trailed after them as they left.

When the double doors of the firehouse closed behind them, she whispered, "You can put me down now."

"I know." He let her slide down his body. "Alone at last, Mrs. Brockman."

"In the Alaskan cold," she said briskly, not quite

able to mask the tremor in her voice. She was Rafe's wife! Joy was a river in her. She walked beside him to their car, waiting for him to unlock it. Then she reached around him, popping the hood to unhook the trickle charger from the battery.

He grimaced. "I always forget about those."

"As long as you don't drive off with them attached."

"Has anyone?" He took the equipment and stowed it in the trunk as she got into the passenger seat.

"Daddy has," she said when he'd slid behind the wheel. "So have my brothers. It almost happened to me."

He laughed. "You're so careful, is that it?"

"I'm just slower to get going, or so Kort says."

"I like your family."

"I'm glad." She hesitated. "Would it matter if you didn't? Or if they didn't like you?"

He shook his head. "So long as it didn't bother you. I can handle anything as long as I belong to you."

If he'd said that she belonged to him, she might've argued. She'd been raised to think of herself as her own person. But he'd said he belonged to her. She could've fallen to her knees in gratitude, because she wanted it so much.

The drive was short. The snow had stopped, and an ineffable silence surrounded them. The streets and roads were tracked with nubby marks of tires past. The eaves of every house drooped snow in voluptuous suspended drifts. The sky was blue-black and scattered with stars. It was a white cocoon of a night.

Cassie felt a wonderful numbness as though she were living through a rapturous dream.

"There's the house," Rafe whispered, letting the car slow.

Cassie stared. Rafe had asked her to avoid going near the Bigelow house, saying he didn't want her to see it until the renovations were finished. It was the same minicastle of stone that she was familiar with, with its classic Gothic lines, the wonderful stone carted from Italy. But she recalled it as tattered and unkempt. Not now. The driveway that had once been pocked with holes was smooth and graded, and someone had cleared it of snow. The porch light provided the only illumination, but it looked like all the overgrown trees and shrubs had been pruned and the wood trim on the house's exterior had been painted.

"It looks wonderful," she said. "Did you have the stone sandblasted?"

"Not yet. I just had a cleanup crew come in and give it a good going-over, inside and outside. In the spring the stone will be cleaned."

"It's lovely."

"I agree."

He pulled up the circular drive and stopped under the portico. "This house could've been placed out on Long Island."

"Yes, it isn't like the others in this area. But the previous owner wanted to make a statement, I suppose."

He laughed. "So do we."

It surprised her when he shifted into drive again and continued along the driveway. She thought he was driving back to the street, but he turned off onto a narrow road alongside the house.

It led to a garage attached to the back of the house. The door opened automatically. Rafe pulled in and parked, shutting off the engine and the lights.

The door shut behind them, and the lights came on in the garage.

"It's warm!" Cassie exclaimed as Rafe helped her from the car.

"Yes. I decided it was easier this way. And since the windmill on the property generates enough power for the energy, I thought it would be environmentally correct."

Cassie eyed him. "You've been listening to my father and some of the others talk about the environment." She sighed, looking around the spacious garage. "They were always careful, but since the oil spill they've been downright obsessed about the care of Alaska."

"I think we need their thinking in Washington. Too little too late won't do it, if we mean to save our space."

"Yes."

She nearly continued the conversation, but he took her arm and led her to a door, and she was overwhelmed by ambivalent sensations of shyness and eagerness.

Once through the door, they walked up two steps and through another door into what Cassie would've described as a canning kitchen. Cupboards lined both sides of the shallow room, with three doors leading from it.

"Like a maze, isn't it?" Rafe said.

"I like it," she said. It was old-fashioned with lots of wood, tightly, cozily built, like a good stout Alaskan house should be.

He reached around her and opened the door to their left. "Those two lead to a storage area." He pushed back the one in front of her.

Cassie walked through the doorways, then stopped in astonishment. They'd come up under a staircase in the middle of a wide hallway. To the left was the front foyer, to the right was the kitchen. All the wood in the hallway was mahogany, burnished to a gleaming chestnut. The chandelier in the foyer was a rainfall of crystal, and it shone brightly.

"Is everything new?" she asked, feeling an odd disappointment at the thought.

"Nothing is new. I thought you'd like to choose whatever furnishings we'll need. Nothing has been altered, only cleaned, buffed, and polished."

"It's a wonderful place."

"I thought so. I only saw photographs of it before I bought it, and it looked like everything was covered with mildew and rot. But I knew it had been beautiful once."

She nodded. "No one had touched it in so long." She felt pain for the neglected old place. Houses had souls too.

"But Lars assured me the foundations were solid. It was worth the price, and I don't regret it."

She smiled at him. "You might regret living through our long winters."

He shrugged. "Actually I like the winter. When I was in college I competed in luge competitions in Lake Placid, and I've spent most of my winters skiing there too."

She blinked. "There's still much I don't know about you."

"You know what's important. And I will do my level best to set everything else straight."

"Will you?" Even the things so deeply hidden they couldn't be dredged up? she wondered. Were there many of those?

"Yes." He watched her. "And are you going to tell me about yourself?"

She looked away. "There will always be parts of us hidden from others, Rafe. As long as we don't hide the facets of our lives that shape us, then we can deal well with each other."

Though intellectually he knew she was right, her admission that she had secrets hurt him. She'd made the same statement in New York. He hadn't passed it off, but he'd felt it was something they would discuss. Now, they were married, and he didn't know why he thought that would change everything, that she'd open up to him completely. He was a fool. Introverted all his life, sharing little of his own "hidden" world with anyone, he should've expected that Cassie might feel the same.

When they'd been together three years ago, he'd had the sensation that she'd been totally open with him at first. After a time she'd become more reserved with him, as their relationship hit rough times. Now, that same closeness was between them again, and it hurt like hell that he might've lost that wonderful openness.

"I guess I can live with that," he said at last.

"I guess we both do, Rafe. Certainly we don't agree on every level—"

"We can work on that." He didn't want her to say any more. "Maybe you'd like to see the rest of the house."

Cassie sensed his withdrawal and nodded reluctantly. She wanted to tell him how she felt about having children, that the hidden part of her would truly be his when he could make that same commitment. They needed to talk it out, thrash out the differences so they could be discarded. He should know how she felt, how strong her resolutions were to have a child of her own, even if he didn't agree. She opened her mouth to tell him that.

He put a gentle hand on her lips. "Not now. It' s our wedding night. Let's explore the house, have something to eat, maybe shower, sit by the fire, sip champagne. . . . What do you think?"

"Sounds wonderful." She'd tell him another time.

Six

Cassie sat up in bed, calm, happy, waiting for Rafe. He was still in the shower. She had the distinct feeling that the cool, self-contained business shark was not so serene at the moment. It made her want to laugh.

"What are you smiling at?"

Rafe stood there, his hair curling and damp, a towel around his shoulders. He wore a robe and pajamas. She chuckled.

He looked down at himself. "Something funny?"

"You. All the time we were together, you couldn't wait to get out of your clothes—"

"I still can't."

"—and most of the time you came to bed stark naked—"

"I'm trying to be considerate."

"Sounds lame, Brockman. I think you're chicken."

"It shows, huh?" He smiled wryly. "And you think it gives you leverage?"

"Some."

He approached the bed, tossing the towel toward a chair. It missed. Discarding his robe, he tossed that too. It missed.

"Great PJs," she said. "Silk?"

"I don't know. I suppose." He climbed into bed and lay down beside her, looking up at her as she sat Indian fashion on top of the covers. "You're dressed."

"Standard uniform for a wedding night. Sheer nightie, though not totally diaphanous, white—"

"Yours is cream."

"An insignificant departure from the norm."

"I see." Rafe's heart thudded up in his throat. She looked so carelessly lovely, so stunningly distracting, so damn collected with her hair spilling over her shoulders, swaying against her cheeks whenever she moved. She'd freed it from its usual neat chignon, and it was like a burnished curtain about her. "I like your hair down. Would you wear it like that all the time?"

Startled, she blinked. "But you must know I can't. It's so thick and straight. It would be flopping in my eyes all the time."

Pleased that he could disconcert her a bit, he grinned. "You can figure out something. You look so great with it loose. Sexy, beautiful, boyish—"

"Boyish?"

"You have the cutest boyish figure I've ever seen. And I love it." He admired the run of blood up her neck. Stretching upward, he let his mouth trace the flow.

"This is shock treatment," she said. "You're doing it to get even. It irked you that I was so calm."

"Not irked, darling, just put off stride by your beauty."

"Liar."

"Uh-uh." He grinned at her, lifting one finger and letting it run from her chin down to the cleavage in her gown. "Of course, you're not completely boyish." His blood heated, and he had to fight for every breath. "You're lovely. And your breasts are perfect."

"Too small," she said, her voice squeaking.

"Just right." He leaned over and kissed the crease between them. "You taste good too." Taking a deep, shuddering breath, he rubbed his cheek against her breast. "I long for you, Cassie."

The quiet declaration almost tipped her over. She touched his hair, unruly and more appealing than the way she usually saw it, well combed and smooth. She dragged her finger down the curve of his ear. "That's a warm thing to say," she said.

He lifted his chin, looking up at her. "Well, I'm warm enough."

She smiled down into his eyes, loving the way her body cradled the upper part of his. "I'm warm."

"I used to wake up at night and think you were there, Cassie. Then I'd lie awake hugging the pillow and hating the emptiness for the rest of the night." His smile was lopsided. "I did a great deal to forget you. Nothing worked, so I gave in to it and bought this house. Once it was ready, I had every intention of coming to Alaska and begging you to marry me. The Cosmo died, and your father told me you'd be coming to Manhattan. I knew I had to try my damnedest then."

Shocked, she could only stare at him. He'd

voiced her pain, her same agony. "I hugged a pillow, too, more times than I could count. And the Alaskan nights seemed so endless. I was lonely," she whispered.

"Lonely? Hell, I was bisected, one part with you, the other part trying to operate at half force."

She leaned over him, her hair waterfalling about them.

"Ahhh, that's one of the things I missed most." He closed his eyes, relishing the closeness. "I wanted to be wrapped in your hair and never let loose."

"Rafe," she sobbed.

"Don't cry, darling. I don't want you to cry."

"Not unhappy." She gulped. "We've said so much." But not all of it. The errant voice tried to trip her out of the beautiful aura they were building. She fought back. Everything couldn't be handled in one moment. Each point would have a time. She'd see to that. She and Rafe had too much to lose.

"You're wandering away," he murmured.

"No. I'm here." She tightened her arms around him.

"Don't leave me."

"I won't."

He turned in her arms, his own sliding around her waist, his mouth pressed to her middle. "Umm, I like the feel of the satin, but your skin is softer."

"I love you."

"I love you too."

No gloss, no frills, no ruffles. Just straight-out feelings with no side trips to flowery excuses or cute ambiguities.

"Let go, love," Rafe whispered. "Let's be one."

"Yes." She didn't know how he moved or maneuvered her down, but all at once she was lying on her back, and he was leaning over her. "Handsome."

"What?"

"I said 'handsome.' That's what you are." When she saw his cheeks redden, she grinned. "I like putting you off balance."

"I like retaliating." He lowered his head and nibbled his way down her neck and chest to her breast. She gasped, then obligingly raised her arms when he lifted her gown over her head.

"This is my favorite way for you to be," he said hoarsely. "And I've waited so long."

"So have I. Cosmo told me I was a fool not to get in touch with you. He was right."

"He told me the same thing." Suddenly he lifted her up, pressing his face to her breasts. "But I'm a fool no longer. I love you and want you."

"I want you too," she said, and pulled his head up to kiss him.

They kissed ravenously, as though they'd been starved for each other for weeks. Their hands explored eagerly, finding all those wonderful places that elicited moans of delight from the other.

"It's like hang gliding," Cassie murmured as he paid homage to her breasts.

"What?" he said hoarsely.

"Making love." She smiled when he laughed. "It is. You know you're there, on earth. Then you're off the cliff, catching a puff, a breeze, the ultimate lift, and it's happening. All the wonder of flying, but not being out of control. No heavy piece of machinery between you and the heavens. Just you, and air, and wonder."

"I like your description." He lowered his head again, his mouth roving her skin as though he'd discovered a new world and wanted to explore every inch.

Cassie clung to him, making soft little sounds in her throat, unable to stem the flood of happiness that rose up in her. She wanted to tell him how she felt, urge him not to stop, make sure he knew how happy he was making her. But words failed as they always did when Rafe and she were caught in the power.

Her body melted against him, sinuous, wanting, needing, desiring, pulsating with the rhythm that had always been theirs. When his hand moved lower, she couldn't restrain her sobbing sigh. She bowed her body as though to give him access.

The throbbing began with his magical fingers as they caressed the soft, damp lips of her body's opening. She tensed when he edged aside the soft, slick flesh and intruded smoothly, beginning a cadence that had her sighing with delight. "Rafe!"

"Yes, darling, I know." He stroked the sensitive nub, feeling her tremble, even as his body began a blissful quaking of its own. He needed her. And he needed her wanting and wet.

Gritting his teeth, he fought back the terrific swell of desire that threatened to envelop him. When her hands trembled over his chest and back, he groaned. "Darling! Don't touch me like that."

"You used to like it."

"I still do. I just can't handle it." He smiled ruefully when she chuckled.

His fingers teased her, until he felt and saw her sharply indrawn breath. "You're so wet, love."

"I'm ready, Rafe," she murmured.

"Not yet." It was his turn to chuckle when she glared at him.

"I should know when I'm ready."

"So you should." As passionately ready as he was, he took the time to brush back her hair, letting his hands linger there. "I love you, Cass."

"I know. I love you."

He pressed his face to breasts, one of his favorite things to do. Kissing her gently, he moved downward, slowly, so as not to miss an inch of her skin.

Pulling frantically on his hair, Cassie tried to make him understand. Words wouldn't do, they wouldn't come. They clogged her throat. Her body began a gentle thrashing that should've made her message clear.

When his tongue intruded gently, her hips bucked, and she almost reared up.

"Shh, sweetheart, I'm loving you."

Again words failed her. The throbbing in her head, the thrumming in her blood, the wild, roaring cacophony of her building passion gave her the sensation of riding the Colorado without a raft. "Rafe! I can't—"

"I'm with you, love." He slid up her body and entered her quickly, taking her as she took him.

They spiraled into a thunderous quiet, a pulsating, pounding serenity. They shared it with each other, and no one else could feel the rampage.

Seconds or eons later, Rafe held his wife tightly against him, his face buried in her neck. She heard his muffled curse.

"Rafe? What is it?"

"I didn't take precautions. But you did, didn't you, Cassie?"

She held him close, tamping down her irritation and disappointment that that was the first thing he said to her after such monumental lovemaking. "Women protect themselves these days, Rafe. We have to."

She hadn't used protection, though. She hadn't even thought about it, and she should have. It wouldn't be fair for her to try to get pregnant when he was so opposed to children. Still, she didn't tell him the truth. She didn't want the disagreement to impose itself on their wonderful languor.

Nonetheless, when he sighed with relief, she couldn't keep silent.

"It wouldn't be the end of the world," she began, "if we had a—"

He put his hand over her mouth. "We haven't discussed this fully, I know that. But until we do, let's not change the status quo. I love you."

"And I love you, Rafe." Studying him carefully, Cassie saw his fears for the first time, the pain and vulnerability. "Rafe, why didn't you tell me about Linnie when we were first together? It was a terrible thing, but she seems to be handling it well."

"I wanted to . . . most of the time. I wanted you to know everything about me . . . and about my parents." He let his head fall forward on her breasts. "There never seemed a good time to tell you."

"And you put off letting me meet your aunt and sister, time after time."

"I did." He exhaled heavily. "A part of me knew you'd understand, sympathize, that you would love Linnie and Aunt Adela on sight." He lifted her hand and kissed it. "I'm trying to deal with my dark side."

"And I'm glad we discussed it, but you can open up to me more fully . . . just as I can with you."

"I want that. Will you tell me about your hidden self?"

"Yes," she said softly. "It's a beginning, isn't it?"

"Yes."

She brushed his hair back from his forehead as he edged up next to her, leaning against the headboard and holding her close. "You were partially right in New York when you said you'd thought I didn't love you as deeply as you loved me. I did love you, but I was afraid to trust you. I told myself that what we had was too thin for permanence, that I couldn't trust you to be warm and open, a full partner. But I've come to realize that I feared what we had. . . . Don't laugh."

"I'm not laughing," he said.

"It was too big, involving every emotion, every facet of my life. I'd given over too much of myself, or so I thought. And when you seemed to pull back from me. . . ."

He touched her cheek. "I'm sorry, darling."

"It wasn't your fault. It was mine. I was afraid, and yet I was enthralled. You pulled me as no one had ever done. The commitment frightened the hell out of me. Even now, I don't know if I was secretly relieved at Cosmo's predicament so that I could run. And I still am not sure if I ran from you or myself."

He was silent for a long moment, then bent down to kiss the corner of her mouth.

"Quite a confession."

"I'll say." She smiled shakily. "But it felt good to say it."

"I know what you mean. I guess I'm glad I wasn't the only one overwhelmed by what had happened to us." He pulled her close, looking deep into her eyes. "I wanted to marry you the night I met you."

"I'll bet that was scary."

"As hell." His smile faded. "From the beginning I wanted you to know about my family, but I put it off. I feared your reaction, and I loved you so much I was afraid to jeopardize what we had. But another part of me couldn't discuss what happened to Linnie, because it made me sick each time I tried." He shook his head. "I should've known what the therapist ended up telling me, that I needed to air my pain, look at it, analyze it, and put it where it belonged, in a back corner of my mind."

"Even then, I knew you had secrets."

"A part of me, the dark side, couldn't conceive of you wanting to stay with me after I told you all the tawdry details." He sighed. "I should have had more faith in you, darling."

"And I should've had the same faith in you . . . and myself. I was afraid too." She shook her head. "It was big, too big, and we weren't big enough."

"Not you, Cass. Me."

"Both of us. I should've had enough faith in our relationship to insist you tell me why you were hiding your family from me. Instead, I fumed in silence, and the resulting rancor helped to part us."

"You came from a lively, loving family. Mine was so far off the norm that it bordered on the fantastic. I can remember our Christmases when Linnie and I were children. Sometimes there'd be something under the tree from our parents, sometimes not. And after that time—"

"What time?" she asked, cuddling close to him.

"I can only describe it as one bad Christmas. Linnie and I were still pretty young."

When he paused again, she lifted her head. "Tell me."

"Linnie and I hurried downstairs . . . and there were whiskey bottles on the floor and a couple of things in paper bags. We thought they were for us. They weren't. The bags had more booze in them, and what I came to realize later was dope. Linnie and I sat under the tree, not saying anything."

"Rafe." She hugged him tight, feeling his anguish, recalling her own wonderful Christmases with her family, the laughter, the kidding, the loving.

"Aunt Adela and Uncle Edward came over early," he went on, "and they found us like that. The next Christmas there were presents under the tree, signed by Mother and Dad. We knew they were from our aunt and uncle." He kissed her forehead. "It's funny about children and their connection to their parents. We were never close to them, but it was such a shock when they died."

Cassie could imagine and feel his pain. Yet despite all that his childhood had lacked, all he had suffered, she knew Rafe to be kind, loving, generous. Genes weren't everything, but she didn't say that.

He kissed her cheek. "What're you thinking?"

"You didn't cause your parents' woes. They

created them. They were the only ones who could stop the roller coaster they were on . . . and they did." She saw how his features contorted, as though the battle he waged was an ongoing one. "I believe that in the end your father understood what he and your mother had done to you and Linnie. Perhaps they even talked about it. I think your father was trying to remove the pain before he and your mother died."

Rafe's smile was hard. "I've forgiven them, Cassie. I had to do that, or I would've never been well. But it's hellish for me to even contemplate passing on such genes to other children."

"Rafe, Rafe, it's not just genes that make us do insane things. People with the best genes will be monsters given the right conditions. An abusive homelife, booze, drugs, an unbridled temper, inflexibility. Not just genes."

"I know. But I also know that defective genes can be passed on to children."

Frustration rose in her, but she tamped it back. One conflict at a time.

"I'm sorry, Cassie, for not telling you about my family before. But I feared I'd lose you." He sighed. "And I did anyway. Cosmo called me a fool so much, I began to think it was my middle name."

"He was wise. And blunt." And Rafe had effectively changed the subject. It was going to be an uphill struggle, she knew, to try to make him change his mind.

"He was the brother I never had," Rafe said softly. "I wanted him to live."

Cassie nodded. "He had so much to offer the world. You saw some of his artwork hanging in my parents' home. And there's more stored away.

We're going to try to find a museum or gallery that would want to display his works permanently. He's really that good."

"And you still talk of him in the present."

"He was such a wonderful part of my life, and my family's. And twice he came to my school and showed the children so many things about drawing. When he played the flute for them, they were enthralled. He was a marvelous musician. One or two of my pupils have shown great promise in music and art, and they talk about Cosmo. I'm going to try to help them when the time comes for school."

"Perhaps we could set up a scholarship fund in Cosmo's name. What do you think?"

Cassie's eyes were moist when she reached up to kiss her husband. "That would be wonderful."

"When you look at me that way, I can't think of anything but making love, wife."

"So? Who's stopping you?"

"Temptress."

"That's me."

He began to kiss her, laughing softly when she became the aggressor. Lying back, he invited her to give full rein to her feelings. He needed her fire, her heat. Little by little, the ice center of him was melting. Only Cassie could do that.

They climbed the lovers' mountain once more, eager, wanting, hot.

January passed swiftly. Cassie moved through each day in a haze of delight, not even feeling the winter's cold. Rafe's love was like a thick comforter she kept wrapped around her. As February began, the days were noticeably longer, with more sunshine and a newness to the crisp air.

On Valentine's Day Rafe insisted she drive home for lunch. He had sandwiches ready, ham and cheese on rye. He gave her a funny card. The diamond pendant pinned to the inside was exquisite, and she kissed him over and over, thanking him and telling him at the same time that he shouldn't have been so extravagant.

"Make up your mind," he said, laughing.

"I can't," she wailed. When he laughed louder, she handed him the card she'd bought for him.

Opening it, he gazed at it for a long moment. On the front of the card was a drawing of a man with a paper bag over his head. Inside it said, "Happy Valentine's to a guy who's good in the sack."

Rafe stared from the card to Cassie and back again.

"Well?" she asked, worried that she'd hurt his feelings.

He looked up slowly, his lips quirking in a grin. "Why, Mrs. Brockman, that's downright lewd." He scooped her into his arms and swung her around and around. "I love it. Let's go upstairs and prove it."

"Fine with me," she said, laughing, then gasped when he carried her up the stairs, two at a time. "Macho Man."

"Eager," he said, a little out of breath. He pushed their bedroom door open with his shoulder and strode to the bed, lying down with her, rather than just placing her there. "Home at last."

She loosened his tie. "You don't go very far every day, just down to that storefront office you're renting."

"But I earn my daily bread by the sweat of my brow. Feel." He pushed his face against her, inhaling her essence, loving it. "And I like that office. It's very up-to-date, with all the electronic equipment that allows me to keep in close touch with New York. Enough about business. I want to make love to my wife."

"I only have about forty-five—"

"Don't talk, woman, disrobe. I'll get you back in time."

She laughed and hugged her husband, kissing him passionately, then eagerly helping him out of his clothes.

"Darling . . . easy," he said as she thoroughly explored his naked body.

"You don't like it?" she asked seductively.

"You know I do. But even though we're hurrying, I don't want to explode too soon, and if you continue . . ."

"I can't help it, you sexy man. You drive me wild."

He grinned. "That's the idea."

She sighed brokenly as his mouth skated over her body, brushing her breasts, then concentrating on the left nipple, sucking, circling it with his tongue.

"You have beautiful skin, Cassie mine," he murmured, then began a lazy, serpentine journey down her body. Crying out, she arched up to him, wordlessly begging him to take her.

Rafe resisted the temptation. Passion had his being vibrating, but he wanted more. He wanted her joy and fulfillment more than he'd ever wanted anything in his life.

He lifted his head, his hair tousled. "You glow

when you smile, Cassie, not just your eyes but your whole body. You're designed for happiness, darling, and you give it off like some sort of wild perfume."

"Poetic," she whispered. She stared into his glinting midnight-blue eyes and knew she was lost forever. His hands slid up and down her, cupping her hips, her breasts, flattening out over her abdomen. He kissed her again and again, building the heat.

Then they took each other in consummate giving.

When Rafe let her off at the school, she turned to him just as she was leaving the car. "I meant to tell you that I might be a little late on Friday. Better take your car to the airport when you go to New York tomorrow. That way you won't be stuck waiting for me if I get tied up. Dr. B.'s a darling, but he always runs late."

Rafe felt a swelling of alarm. "Are you ill?"

"Not at all. It's just that our school system demands a yearly physical. Routine, pard." She leaned over and kissed his cheek.

He turned his head, catching her lips with his. "You have to be healthy."

"Go to work," she said, scoffing at his concern. "And watch out for the ice. The thaw and freeze we had have created some interesting patches."

"Thank you, Mama. But remember, I used to live in Lake Placid at times. I understand ice."

"Alaskan ice is better and different," she said saucily, getting out of the car.

He didn't leave until she rounded the corner of the school and was out of sight.

Cassie sat on the examining table in the doctor's office, dressed only in a hospital gown that didn't quite cover all her bare spots. Surely Dr. Barnum was done, she thought. Physicals were so boring. She was 100 percent healthy.

She was about to jump down off the table and begin dressing, when the door opened. Dr. Barnum walked in and said, "Since you said you haven't been to a gynecologist recently, Cassie, maybe I should do a quick pelvic exam. I've asked Millie to come in—good, here she is."

Cassie greeted the nurse, who kept a discreet distance during the pelvic exam.

Afterward, when he told Millie she could leave the room, Cassie noticed the nurse's smile. "Yes, Doctor, I imagine you and Cassie will want to have a private talk," she said.

When they were alone, Cassie frowned at the GP. "What is it?"

Dr. Barnum smiled. "Everything's fine, Cass. But I'm a little surprised. Mary was of the opinion that you two were going to wait awhile."

"For what?"

"To have a family."

Cassie almost fell off the table. "What're you saying?" She held up a hand when he opened his mouth. "No, don't say anything yet."

Dr. Barnum put down his clipboard. "Cassie, haven't you talked your pregnancy over with your husband?"

"How could I?" she muttered. "I didn't know about it."

"What? Surely you noticed that you'd missed your menstruation."

"I have irregular periods," she said, shrugging. "Once I went for two months."

"Yes, yes, but surely you questioned it this time. You're married."

"I know. It just didn't register."

He sighed. "Well, I'm sure you and your husband—"

"Rafe!"

Dr. Barnum looked taken aback at her vehemence. "Yes, that's his name—"

"Dr. Barnum, I don't want you to tell anyone about this."

"Cassie! I don't discuss my cases with anyone."

"Yes, sure, of course you don't. Excuse me, will you, I should get dressed."

"All right," the doctor said reluctantly. "Everything checks out normally. You might want to use our phone to call Dr. Anderson. She's a fine young woman and an excellent ob/gyn. You should make an appointment right away."

"What? Oh, right. Sure. I'll do that."

"Cassie? Is something wrong? Don't you want the baby? There are things . . ." he began hesitantly.

"No, no. I want the baby." I'm just not sure my husband does, she added silently. In fact, I'm sure he doesn't. "I guess I was a little surprised by it all. We were going to put our family off for a time . . . but now . . . well, the plans have changed."

The doctor smiled, not trying to hide the relief he felt. "Good. Now, you can get dressed."

Cassie dressed in a daze. Had she put her shoes on the right feet? Had she put on her underwear?

Ridiculous. She was making mountains out of molehills. Rafe would understand. Even as she thought it, she pictured the confrontations they'd had on that very subject. Rafe would prefer to adopt rather than have their own! What was the difference when all was said and done? she thought. The same problems could arise with an adopted child as with a biological one. But, Lord, what a tangle. Would Rafe leave her because of this?

By the time she reached the outer office, she felt she'd been torn six ways to the middle. Millie beamed when she asked to use the phone to call Dr. Anderson.

"I could tell the news from Dr. Barnum's face when he did the pelvic—he gets a certain look when a patient's pregnant," Millie said. "Congratulations, Cassie. I'm happy for you."

"Thank you, Millie." She would have to tell Rafe now. Millie had the kindest heart in the region, but she also had a built-in need to be the first one with news. Not all the doctor's chiding kept her totally in check. She'd never been known to betray a confidence or his confidentiality, but she'd consider birth good news, and she'd want to spread it. Cassie knew she could tell her to keep it to herself, but she couldn't bear to face the wellspring of curiosity that would almost burst from Millie if she did. So she smiled, said nothing, and walked out of the office.

Rafe was coming back from Manhattan that evening. And she'd have to face him with it. Would he hate her? Maybe. He didn't want their natural children. And she wasn't going to get an abortion. She wanted the baby . . . his baby and hers. She recalled their wedding night when they'd had such an earnest discussion about their hidden sides, how they would no longer hold back from each other, how they'd talk about whatever came along, so that there'd never be the misunderstandings that had separated them the first time. Somehow that loving confrontation, the covenants sworn between them, seemed a little thin now when they were faced with parenthood. A baby! She could've jumped for joy. If a part of her heart was heavy because of what Rafe would say, it didn't dampen her happiness. One step at a time, she told herself.

Although she was due back at school, her car seemed to have a mind of its own, heading instead toward her parents' house. She regretted her impulse when she pulled into the driveway. She couldn't tell her parents that Rafe didn't want children. And she shouldn't tell them anything until she'd talked to her husband.

She sat behind the wheel for long moments, staring out the windshield. Spring was coming. And she'd have a baby in the fall. On Christmas Eve she might be alone with the baby. And Christmas Eve was their very special day. She would die without him. But she'd live for her baby.

"Daydreaming, dear?"

Startled, Cassie looked up from where she'd rested her forehead on the wheel. "Adela. How are you?"

"Better than you, I think." She opened the door and took hold of one of Cassie's arms. "Why don't you come in? The wind's picking up, and it's getting blustery. I could make some tea. The boys aren't home yet, and Linnie went with your mother and father to meet the Cadwells."

"Yes. Mina and Del. They're cousins of Mother's." Cassie felt weighted down, held in the car seat.

"Come along," Adela said softly. "We can talk."

Cassie fought the tears, but they bubbled out anyway.

Adela said no more. She reached over and pulled the keys from the ignition, then led Cassie into the house. "Your mother and father insist they're not sick of me," she chattered, "but I'll be glad for their sakes when my own place is finished. I like it so much in Valdez. And I've made so many lovely friends." She urged Cassie down the hall to the kitchen. "We're all alone, dear, so why don't you sit down and I'll get us some tea. I could use—"

"I didn't mean to come," Cassie blurted out.

"Yes, you did. Because you knew that you'd be safe, that you could talk, that you could . . . unburden yourself." Adela all but pushed her into a chair, then whirled away to the stove to put the kettle on. She set out the tea things and sat down beside Cassie. "Tell me."

"I'm . . . I'm pregnant."

Silence.

Adela sighed. "I won't pretend I don't know that Rafe's dead set against having any of his own children. As private a person as he is, he's made no secret of how he feels about that."

Cassie nodded, dabbing at her eyes. "I can't and won't have an abortion. I have to make choices too. No woman should be forced to bear children, especially if it's conceived in a rape. But this is my child, of the man I love, and I want it."

"Of course you do." Adela looked down at the table. "I'll talk to Rafe—"

"No, that's my job," Cassie said, her voice shaky.

"He loves you, Cassie. That I know."

Cassie nodded, trying to smile.

"Then give him a chance. Make him see how deeply you feel about this."

Cassie sighed. "He's adamant. He's never said he blames his parents for what happened to Linnie, but I think he does. I think he has the morbid idea that he comes from a bad seed, that whatever caused his parents' irresponsible behavior is a genetic flaw."

The kettle whistled, and Adela got up to make the tea. "You had to know them to understand his pain," she said as she poured water into the two mugs. "They were like nasty adult caricatures of children. They were hedonistic to an alarming degree, and they saw nothing wrong with being indifferent to their children and feeding every desire that arose, whether it was wholesome or not. More than likely it wasn't." Adela shook her head, setting Cassie's tea down in front of her. "In their own way I think they loved their children. But their indulgences became addictions, and they could no longer control what they did, or what avenues their depraved tastes would take. Little by little they even lost their friends, except for the hangers-on who wanted to catch some windfall from their spending sprees."

Cassie looked morose. "They sound most unlikable."

"They weren't. When sober and straight, they were charming, gentle, and they used to laugh all the time. Not near the end, of course. Then, even I couldn't like them. And I certainly feared for Rafe and Linnie."

"Linnie could've been destroyed."

Adela nodded. "Instead, she made it, and Rafe became the damaged one."

Cassie stared at his aunt. "Yes, that's true. He is wounded, isn't he?"

"He's a fighter, too, and he won't be destroyed. But he's scarred, damn them. Badly scarred." Tears misted her eyes. "You're his salvation, Cassie. Don't give up on him."

Startled, Cassie opened her mouth, closed it, then opened it again. "But I wouldn't abandon him. He'll dump me."

Adela shook her head.

"He won't?"

"He's afraid, Cassie, not just of having a child. I think his real fear is of losing you. He could do that in childbirth."

"But—but I'm completely healthy." Back straightening, Cassie began to have hope. "Nothing is going to happen to me. My mother had all of us like falling off a horse, as she described it. She always said Daddy was in much worse shape."

Adela chuckled. "I'm sure of that. Your father dotes on your mother."

Cassie smiled. "He does. But what about Rafe?"

"What about him? I think it comes down to whether you think you can fight this inner bogey of his. A little shadow of a person inhabits his soul, Cassie. If you and Rafe can't eradicate him, he'll eventually destroy what you have."

"I can beat any demon," Cassie said, her body stiffening as though she were preparing for a fight.

Adela studied her, then smiled. "I think you might."

"Not might. Will. No one has the right to interfere between Rafe and me." She rose to her feet. "I thought he might want to leave me. You say he won't—"

"He won't."

"Then I'll fight him on this. I'm going home."

Adela laughed shakily. "You've got a battle glint in your eye."

Cassie looked over her shoulder. "I think that's an understatement."

"Oh, Cassie, I'm proud of you. Rafe will be a wonderful father, you know."

Cassie turned around, nodding fiercely. "I know he will. He's very compassionate."

"Yes. And he needs you."

"I know. I need him, Adela, his warmth, his light, his goodness." She scowled. "But sometimes I could bash him for being obstinate."

"His uncle was the same way. My darling Edward was so accommodating, unless he got a bee in his bonnet. Then he was a brick wall."

"Rafe's a brick wall about having children." The smile trembled off her face. "I love him, but I'm afraid."

"Don't be, child. He loves you madly."

Cassie swiped the tears from her face. "He'd better. We're married, and I won't let him get away."

"He's a fool about this. Would it help if I hold him down and you beat on him?"

"Good idea." Cassie straightened her shoulders.

"Cosmo would be ashamed of me, giving up on Rafe. He always told me Rafe was the best there was. I said I believed him, but I haven't shown it. I will now."

Adela stood in the center of the kitchen, watching as Cassie strode down the hall to the front door. "Go get 'em, Cassie. Give 'em hell, Rafe and anybody who gets in your way." She wiped away a few tears that had trickled down her own cheeks, then abruptly started after Cassie. "Wait! Cassie, Rafe isn't home from New York—"

"I know, I know," she said blithely, hurrying out the door to her car.

Adela chased after her. "Then where are you going?"

"To get my warbonnet on."

Seven

Rafe stepped out of the plane, inhaling the bite of Alaskan air. He was glad to be back. He flew to New York at least twice a month, staying for several days. Each time it was harder to leave Alaska, and each time he was more eager to return.

He saw the man leaning against the wall of the airport lounge as soon as he entered the area. "Lars?"

His brother-in-law approached him, not smiling.

"Cassie? Is something wrong?" Rafe's heart squeezed dry, blood rushing from his head. He gripped Lars's arm.

"Easy, Rafe. Nothing's wrong with her . . . physically."

"What? Has something happened?" Rafe's voice rose, and he didn't care that passersby eyed him strangely.

"Take it easy."

"Tell me."

"Lower your voice. My mother will tear a strip off us if we create a scene in the airport." He started toward the exit, Rafe striding along beside him, scowling. Lars went on, "Did I ever tell you about the time she lambasted us good when we tore down the goalposts at the school after our big game? See, they'd just put them up, and it'd cost the school quite a bit of money. So—"

"Dammit, Lars. What the hell are you talking about? I want to know about Cassie."

They reached the exit, where Willie and Kort were waiting. Rafe stared at the three brothers, panic rising.

"Something's happened to her, hasn't it? Tell me, or so help me God, I'll tear this damn terminal down brick by brick."

Lars shook his head when his brothers tried to take hold of Rafe. "All right, all right," he whispered, glancing left and right. "We're not even supposed to be here. We told Mother we were picking you up, but she said—"

"I don't give a damn about that. Tell me about Cassie," Rafe said roughly, facing the semicircle of brothers-in-law.

"Let's get out of here," Lars said. "We can go somewhere else and talk."

"How about Owney's?" Willie suggested. "It's not that far away."

Lars nodded. "Willie and I will go with you, Rafe. Kort, you follow us in my truck." He tossed his younger brother the keys.

Kort nodded once. "I gotta get home early. I promised Linnie."

Willie grimaced as Kort trotted away. "He's turned into quite a lamb."

"Reminds me of Rafe."

"Very funny, Lars," Rafe said. "Let's get out of here." He glared at his laughing brothers-in-law, but relief set in too. Cassie's brothers wouldn't be making jokes if there was something terribly wrong with her. She wasn't injured, she wasn't sick. But something definitely was up.

The ride took forever.

The ride took ten minutes.

Lars tried to make conversation in between giving Rafe directions. "How was Manhattan?"

"The same."

"Business taken care of?"

"Yes."

"Real estate must be slow. Slow times."

"Yes."

Lars sighed and looked out the passenger window.

Rafe burst out of the car after he'd parked it, facing Lars over the roof of the vehicle. "I don't like this."

"We're just trying to help, Rafe."

Before Rafe could say anything more, Willie got out of the car, slamming the back passenger door. "Let's go. I need a beer."

"Me too," said Lars, jerking his head at Rafe. "This won't take long."

Kort pulled up behind them in Lars's truck. He got out and smiled at Rafe.

Rafe strode past him angrily, pushing open the door, then pausing while his eyes adjusted to the dim light inside the local hangout.

The decor was early junkyard. The bar, a badly

scraped and scarred section of oak that extended the length of the narrow room, had a distinct sag in its middle. Cobwebs swung desultorily from the yellowish lights overhead. Along the wall opposite the bar were dingy high-backed booths, their wood chipped and dented. The floor was linoleum, well worn and uneven. In some places the edges were torn and ragged, an obstacle course for the overindulgent. Owney's needed a face- and body-lift.

From behind the bar Owney eyed the four men warily. "Hey boys, what'll ya have?"

"Whozzat, Owney?" asked one of the men hunched on a barstool.

"Just the Nordstroms, Doley. No business of yours, so keep your mouth shut. They can be a handful if they're riled." Owney squinted across the room, where the men had taken seats at the lone table in the center of the floor. "I don't know the other guy except by sight. He's married to Cassie Nordstrom."

Doley Petman frowned. "Cassie and her sisters is hoity-toity."

"And they can be as tough as their brothers," Owney said dryly. "But they never come in this place, so they don't worry me."

"How come they look so pros-prus?" Doley asked. "Huh, boys?" The disreputable group of riggers and fishermen scattered along the bar nodded and shrugged. "Times is tough all over the United States. Jobs're scarcer than hen's teeth. No different in Alaska. So, how come they look like the livin' is easy?"

Owney gritted his teeth and attempted to re-move Doley's beer glass, but the man was too quick for him. Doley swallowed the contents in one gulp, then slammed it down on the bar, eyeing the new arrivals balefully.

"Cut it out, Doley," Owney said. "Everyone would like the good old days back when the fishing was good before the oil spill—"

"Before the encroachers began screaming about wanting their piece of the pie," a rigger said broodingly. "When we took care of our places and didn't have big business buying us out."

"Yeah," Doley said, belching. "We're getting mad about it too. Free men, free choices. That's us, that's Alaska. But we got no jobs. Give me a beer, Owney."

"No." Owney turned away to wait on someone else.

Doley eyed the freshly poured beer ordered by one of the pool players. He reached out and hooked it toward him.

"They look pretty fancy, huh, Doley," one of his cronies said.

"Yeah." Doley squinted at the new arrivals. "I don't like the Nordstroms. They're as down-and-out as the rest of us, but they act like their rusty trucks is Caddys."

He swung around on his stool, winking at his buddies. "Well, well, if it isn't the Nordstroms and their fancy brother-in-law. Ain't his shoes shiny, boys?" When his friends sniggered, Doley beamed. It might be a fun afternoon after all.

"Doley," Lars said, nodding to the man.

Willie and Kort eyed the group, silently.

Frustrated, Rafe didn't notice the growing tension. "Talk to me, Lars. I'm getting damn sick—"

"Gonna order lemonade for the New York

slicker?" Doley asked. He looked around, preening when his cronies chuckled.

"Maybe we should leave," Willie said softly. "Or I might just take Petman apart."

"Hell, no," Rafe said. "I've had all the jerking around I'm going to take, and I'm not moving until you tell me what's going on with my wife—"

"Keep your voice down," Lars said, glancing up as Doley left his stool.

"What's that I hear?" Doley asked, swaggering over to their table. "Is the big shot's bride giving him trouble? Maybe the kid ain't his." Doley balanced on the balls of his feet, his body telegraphing his eagerness for a fight. His voice, too, was intentionally provocative.

"You insulted my sister," Willie said through his teeth, his hands clenching into fists.

Lars grabbed his brother's arm, though his own face was flushed with anger. "We didn't come here to fight."

Rafe half rose from his chair, facing Doley Petman, but Lars pushed him down again.

"What the hell is he saying?" Rafe asked. "Is he talking about my wife? What kid?"

"He's a jerk," Kort said, standing. "And I'm going to shove his teeth down his throat."

"Shut your mouth, punk," Doley said. "You're still wet behind the ears."

"You—"

Rafe shot up, grabbing Kort's shoulders before he could launch himself at Doley. "Cut it out. What the hell did he mean about the kid?"

Lars eyed Doley and his crew, then glanced at Rafe. He'd have to talk fast; things were getting out of hand. "I said keep your voice down. Cassie was going to tell you, but in this area word spreads fast. No doubt Dr. B. told his nurse, and she's the biggest gossip—"

"Hey," Doley interrupted, "the big shot didn't know about his wife being knocked up. That's a—"

Whatever Doley was going to add wasn't finished.

With a roar Rafe threw himself at Doley, rage and perplexity propelling him. He hit Doley like a juggernaut, taking him down to the floor.

With a roar Doley's cronies leaped at Rafe.

"Damn!" Lars said. "Mom will have my eyes for this." With that, he threw himself into the melee.

"So will Cassie," Willie muttered, before grabbing a tattered shirt collar, bringing back his ham-sized fist, and letting fly.

"Don't tell Linnie," Kort said, smiling. Then he leaped at two men who were about to join the fray.

"Dammit! Stop it!" Owney yelled, leaping over the bar. "Don't break my window again. Buster, call the cops," he shouted to his swamper.

The bar was filled with a jumble of bodies, yelling, cursing, the crashing of glass and the clattering of breaking chairs. Every man there joined in the fight. Many were out of work, and the fighting was a welcome diversion from their frustrations and worries.

Few heard or heeded the approaching sirens.

Owney's window went out again as Doley and one other were tossed through it.

Owney's wail could be heard in concert with the sirens.

Cassie stayed late at school. She had two students after classes, then a conference with a parent. It was dusk when she finally left. Glancing at her watch as she walked to her car, she figured she had enough time to go to the grocery store before Rafe was due home. Grinning, she calculated that she'd known about the baby for seven hours. She was still dazed and thrilled.

At the store she picked up some lobsters. Rafe loved them, and so did she. She wanted them to have a good dinner, relax with a cappuccino afterward, then she'd tell him about the baby.

She saw her mother as she was coming out of the store. "Hi, Mom," she called.

Mary hurried over to her. "How are you feeling, dear?" Mary bit her lip. "Millie called me, you know. . . ."

Cassie shook her head, laughing. "I'm sure Millie's called half of Valdez by now. Mom, you know I wouldn't hide anything from you. But I wanted to tell Rafe first and—"

"I understand dear. And I never thought you were hiding anything. After all, you just found out."

"Yes. I was shocked."

Mary smiled. "Every one of you surprised me."

Cassie laughed again, and was about to answer when two police cars went by. "Gosh, I hope no one was hurt in an accident."

"The highways are getting worse," Mary said, watching the speeding cars out of sight. "Why don't you come over to the house now, and I'll give you that recipe Dinsy Lapper gave me for morning sickness. Her Swedish grandmother gave it to her, and it's wonderful."

Cassie didn't want to take any time away from preparing her dinner, but she figured she could use the potion, and she could see her mother was anxious about her. "All right, but I can only stay a minute. Rafe might be home already."

The phone was ringing as Cassie and her mother walked into the Nordstroms' house. Cassie followed Mary into the kitchen, where her father had answered the phone. "Hi, Dad," she mouthed to him, then stared in surprise as the smile left his face and his jaw dropped.

"Yes, I understand," he said. "I'll be right there. Thank you. Yes, we have a lawyer."

"Lawyer?" her mother said, turning from the counter, where she was unloading her groceries. "Why do we need one, dear?"

Cassie felt the same tightening anxiety she read on her mother's face.

Helborg coughed, then walked over to his wife, patting her on the shoulder. "Now, dear, boys will be boys."

Mary closed her eyes. "What did they do?"

"They've been arrested for fighting at Owney's bar," Helborg said quietly, the smile falling off his face when he turned to Cassie. "It seems they busted his front window."

"All of them?" Mary croaked, leaning back against the counter. "They're too old for this nonsense."

"All of whom?" Linnie asked brightly, coming into the kitchen, unzipping her down coat. "I found the most wonderful material. . . ." Her voice trailed off as she stared at the three immobile persons. "Is it Kort? Has something happened?" She looked frightened, which wasn't surprising. She and Kort had got engaged a week earlier.

"No, dear, no one's hurt," Helborg assured her. "The boys have just been in a brawl. They're . . . ahem, in jail."

"All of them," Mary whispered.

Helborg turned to Cassie. "Including Rafe."

"What?" Linnie and Cassie exclaimed, just as Adela walked into the kitchen.

"I heard voices," she said, "and I have such good news. My home is— What is it? Is something wrong?"

"All of them, including Rafe," Mary said softly, pulling her coat back on. "Call the lawyer, dear."

"What happened?" Adela asked.

"They're in jail," Linnie said, sinking into a chair. "All of them, Rafe too. They were fighting in a bar."

"Rafe?"

"Now, Adela," Cassie said. "It's all—"

Laughter belled out of Adela, peal after peal of it. "I love it. I insist on going with you."

Linnie glared at her aunt. "It's not funny. Kort could've been hurt." Her lips tightened. "And if he's not hurt, we're going to have a talk. Boy, are we going to talk."

"So will Rafe and I," Cassie said, then she whirled to face her father. "He wasn't hurt, was he?"

Helborg shrugged. "Nothing serious. Just some bruises. And Willie has a broken nose."

"Serves him right," Cassie said with relish.

"Cassie!" Mary said.

"We should go," Helborg said, taking Mary's arm.

"Helborg, I want you to talk to them . . . very seriously."

"I will, love. Let's go."

"Linnie and I will ride with Cassie," announced Adela, still chuckling. "I wouldn't miss this for the world."

Linnie looked pained. "It isn't funny."

"Damn right it isn't," Cassie said.

"Oh, but it is," Adela whispered, her eyes going heavenward. She had a feeling all her prayers had been answered.

The court area of the Justice Building was jammed with people, sweaty and flustered, blustering loudly or muttering angrily. The overhead fan in the large, domed room wasn't enough to dissipate the heavy body smells that wafted from the holding cells.

When the bailiff stood and faced the crowd to announce the session, and the door behind the judge's bench opened, the crowd simmered down to mere mumbles. The judge sat, struck his gavel once, and there was a shuffling silence.

"Any disturbance in my court and I'll have it cleared." He glanced at the bailiff and nodded tiredly.

More than a dozen men marched single file into the courtroom. Faces colored with darkening bruises and some cuts, they glanced at the spectators, then faced the judge.

The judge leaned forward, looking at each man in turn before speaking. "Now what we have here are classic cases of arrested development, on the group plan. And it annoys me that you overgrown boys take up this court's time with your silly games. Next time take out your frustrations on video games." His caustic voice droned on, letting everyone there know that he wasn't about to whitewash the incident.

As the various attorneys rose to enter their clients' pleas, Cassie stared at Rafe, or at least at the one side of him that was visible to her. His usually impeccably neat appearance was in total disarray, from his messy hair to his rumpled suit, torn shirt, and scuffed shoes. His tie was missing. Her heart squeezed as she surveyed the damage to his handsome face. One eye was completely closed and a bandage covered half his forehead. His lips were swollen, raw, and sore-looking. More than once he looked back at her, his expression inscrutable. Anger warred with pity inside her. She wanted to cosset him . . . and kill him. Anger was getting the upper hand. Warring with the motley crew at Owney's could have resulted in serious injury.

When Adela tittered as the Nordstroms' attorney rose, Linnie and Cassie glared at her.

Mary sighed. Helborg held her hand.

The judge ordered the miscreants to step forward, one by one admonished them sternly, fined them, and waved them back in line.

When it was over, the men then had to face their families.

Voices rose, pained and angry.

"How could you?"

"Fool. As though we have enough money for your fighting."

"Does it hurt?"

As people began leaving, more than one brawler

went up to Rafe and shook his hand. Out in the hall the three brothers and Rafe faced their family.

Lars drew in a deep breath, staring at his mother from his one open eye. "Now, Mom—"

"Don't you say another word, Lars Helborg. You're the oldest, and you should've stopped this." She stared at each one in turn, including Rafe. "I'll not have any more of this."

Four heads nodded.

"Come along, then, we'll have to treat your bruises."

"I'll have more to say when we reach home," Helborg said.

Four heads nodded.

Adela walked up to them as Helborg and Mary left. "Did you win?"

Rafe tried to smile, but his mouth hurt too much.

Lars, Willie, and Kort nodded.

"I thought so. The others looked worse than you did. But why did I see some of them shake Rafe's hand?"

"They were thanking him for paying all the fines," said Willie, his one hand covering his nose.

"We won, though," Kort said. He grinned, then flinched when his split lip stretched.

"Did you?" Linnie said sweetly. "Let's go home." She took Cassie's proffered keys. "I'll drive."

Kort stopped smiling. "Now, Linnie, honey, it wasn't—"

"I'm not talking in this public place," she told him, and stalked off.

"Aww, Linnie . . ." Kort hurried after her.

Lars grimaced at Cassie and followed Kort.

"You don't have to worry about Rafe, Cass,"

Willie said. "He knows about the baby, and he didn't take any crap from Petman. Oh, my nose hurts."

"Good," Cassie said unfeelingly. She lifted her chin when her brother scowled at her before following the others. Alone with Rafe, she faced him squarely.

"How are you feeling, Cassie?" he asked hesitantly. It was obvious she was spoiling for a fight.

"Better than you, I'd say."

"I can explain," he began, then stopped. He shouldn't let her get excited. Women's blood pressure rose easily when they were pregnant. He'd read that somewhere. He should've researched the whole condition thoroughly. Now, he would. He opened his mouth to tell her that, but she spoke first.

"Shall we go? Your car's in the back, they told me. It was impounded. How wonderful."

He studied her. "You're angry."

"Really? Why would I be? Finding out that my husband is a common street brawler should make me proud, shouldn't it? You're so macho, just what a healthy American woman would want. Yes?"

"No. Now, listen, Cass, it wasn't like that. And you shouldn't raise your voice when—"

"Raise my voice?"

"Now, you're shouting."

"Me? I never shout."

"Fine. We'll go home. You can shout there."

"I . . . do . . . not . . . shout."

A court attendant appeared beside them. "Do you mind taking your squabbles down the hall? You're upsetting the court." He reached out to take Cassie's arm, and she slapped his hand away.

"Watch it, buster."

The attendant looked taken aback.

"She's pregnant," Rafe said.

"Oh. Sorry, ma'am. My wife was just as tetchy when she was that way. But could you keep it down a bit? It disturbs the judge." The man smiled and walked back into the courtroom.

"Tetchy?" Cassie exclaimed. "Did he say I was tetchy?"

"Now, Cassie, honey, don't upset yourself." Rafe took her elbow gingerly, waiting to be swatted.

"I . . . am . . . never . . . tetchy," she said, head up, color high. She stalked toward the exit, Rafe at her side.

"I want to explain to you," he told her carefully, caught between amusement and vexation that she should be so put out with him.

She glanced at him but didn't slacken her pace. "That should be interesting."

She stopped suddenly, and he almost cannoned into her. "Why were you in that part of town with my brothers?"

"They picked me up at the airport."

"Now that's rich."

"It's the truth. They wanted to tell me about the baby."

"And they didn't think you'd hear about it from your wife?"

"Well, yes, I suppose they did . . . but they were trying to cushion the shock of my finding out," he said lamely.

"Hah! And that's why you started a fight at Owney's?"

"Not exactly."

"Do go on."

"I was upset. . . ." He was talking to air. Cassie was heading for the exit again. "Aren't you going to listen?"

"No, but you are, as soon as we get home."

"Now, who's macho?" he muttered.

"I heard that."

"Cass, you're not really that angry, are you?"

She wasn't, but she was trying to work herself into a snit. She had the bizarre sensation that it would be good for their marriage. Maybe one day she'd figure that out.

After some signing, some details, and very little conversation with the man at the pound, they were in Rafe's car and heading home. Cassie driving.

"I wasn't impaired, you know," Rafe said. "I hadn't even gotten a drink—"

"Wonderful. You don't need the stimulation of booze to fight. You can wade in any time, with just a word or gesture to fire you up."

"I'm not like that. You know me—"

"Hah! I thought I did."

"I don't generally fight. But this time I had cause—"

"Just another little tidbit of information about the man I married. He's a bully."

"Cassie, listen. I didn't know about the baby."

"I know that. I was going to tell you after our lobster dinner. Not that you would've been happy about it—"

"I am happy!" he shouted.

"You sound it," she said caustically.

"Look, I know I sounded terrible to you when I said I didn't want any children of our own—"

"You would've sounded bad to any woman."

"All right, I'll admit it was stupid. Hey, watch out for that car."

"I know what I'm doing. I don't need you to tell me how to drive."

"Sorry." He sank back in his seat, watching her. "I missed you."

"Bull."

"Cassie, I've had a great deal of time to think about what I said to you—"

She shook her head. "Not now. I'd rather talk when we get home."

When she pulled into their heated garage and stopped the car, he turned to her. "Cass, I—"

She got out of the car and stalked into the house. He found her in the kitchen. She'd already removed her coat and boots and was putting the kettle on.

"Cass! Dammit, I want to talk."

"So do I. But I want some tea."

"Oh. Sure. Let me make it. You can sit down and—"

"No, I'll do it."

Neither spoke as they waited for the water to boil. Cassie measured tea leaves into the pot, then poured in the hot water. While the tea steeped, she got out two mugs, the milk, and sugar. She poured tea into one mug, added milk, and walked out of the kitchen. She headed for the living room, knowing Rafe was right on her heels. She walked to the middle of the room and turned to face him.

"Now. Why in blazes were you at Owney's?"

Rafe opened his mouth, closed it, and sipped his

TWAS THE NIGHT • 145

tea. He flinched when the scalding liquid touched his cut lip, then looked away from her. "You're pregnant." He carelessly took another gulp and burned his mouth.

"That's why you were at Owney's? Because I'm pregnant?"

"No . . . Yes . . . No." He moved his shoulders as though to shift a burden he had atop them. "Lars met me at the airport. He wanted to break the news to me that it was all over Valdez that you were pregnant—"

"Not all over. Millie isn't that powerful."

"I guess your brothers sensed something was up between us." He smiled crookedly. "I don't know if they were trying to protect you or me."

"Go on."

"So we stopped at that bar, and everyone there knew you were pregnant." When her lips tightened, he grimaced, nodding. "Lars wanted to leave, but I didn't want to wait any longer to find out what he had to tell me. Then Petman made some remark—"

"Doley Petman is a loser. He always has been. Nobody listens to him, except for his hat-size-IQ cronies."

"Yeah, well, I wasn't thinking too straight. He knew about it, and I wanted to kill him because I wanted to know first—"

"What?" Hope and mirth spiraled through her. "You started a fight because you weren't the first to know about the baby?"

He looked down, sipping his tea, and she watched the run of blood up his neck. She sat down on the sofa, covering her mouth with her hand.

He caught the gesture and narrowed his eyes at her. "It wasn't funny," he muttered.

"Oh, but it is."

"Cassie." He took a few steps closer to her, setting his mug down. "I love you so much, and I couldn't handle that I was happy as hell you were pregnant. And yet, I'm still scared of losing you. It was like being tipped upside down and shaken. But I didn't get a chance to sort out what I was feeling, because that fool made his remarks." Rafe shifted uncomfortably. "It felt real good to hit him."

Cassie stared up at him. "I don't think Alaska's been good for you. Since you've come up here, you've developed a belligerent streak. You're ready to fight at the drop of a hat."

He shrugged. "Personally I think Alaska's been good for me. I don't hide how I feel anymore. It feels good." He took another step toward her. "I don't believe in fighting, and I'll never believe that war accomplishes anything. But it felt damn good to pop Doley Petman, and it was worth the lumps to take him down. I won't hide that from you."

"You haven't been hiding a lot of things," she murmured.

"I love you, Cassie. And I'm sure as hell not going to hide that. It's a real change for me. I didn't want our baby. And I was prepared to do anything to prevent having one."

"So you said."

He saw the flash of pain in her eyes. Stepping closer, he lifted his arms, then stopped, moving back again. "Cass, I was a fool."

She lifted her chin, staring at him. "You were."

"I know you want this baby—"

"I do. And I'm going to keep it."

"I want to keep it too," he said softly. "Will you keep me, so that I can prove it to you?"

She felt as though she were swaying atop a tall, tall flagpole, reaching for the sun. "I won't change my mind," she whispered.

"I know." He took a deep breath. "Let's make a bargain. Give me a month. Let me show you how much I want to stay with you and the baby. Will you do that?"

"Do you think you can convince me in a month? What if I don't believe you then?" With all her heart she wanted to believe him, keep him.

He smiled fleetingly. "Then it's up to you. You can tell me to get out, leave you alone." It took all he had to say that. He couldn't lose her. It would be like cutting out his heart. "Everything I have will always be yours, Cass. You know that. If I have to get an apartment in Valdez to make you comfortable, I'll do it."

"Wouldn't you go back to Manhattan?"

He shook his head. "I'm going to live here, hopefully with you . . . or without you. But I'm here to stay."

They stared at each other, fighting their fears, trying to come to terms with what was happening to them.

"A month, you say?"

He nodded.

"A month it is."

Eight

Cassie would've gone mad without school and her music. She played her flute for hours on end at home, finding it ironic that her skill was being honed even finer with such concentrated work-outs that frustration forced on her.

And school. Her pupils were a godsend. The children with their myriad problems, their constant badgering for attention, helped keep her fears at bay. If Rafe left her, she'd be back in limbo. And this time there'd be no Cosmo to tease her into smiles, to laugh at her worries, to encourage her to do the right thing, to insist that she love Rafe and be with him.

One morning she was rehearsing the orchestra for their spring concert, and it was going badly. She tapped her baton for them to stop. "Let's try it again."

"Without Dan on piano it doesn't sound good, Mrs. Brockman," Chloe Arndt said plaintively.

"And he's been throwing up for two days. My mother said so."

"Yes, well, we'll just have to try to get along without him today." She could accompany them on the piano herself, but sometimes when she was at the keyboard, her pupils lost their concentration. There was something about standing in front of them with a baton that kept their concentration on the music.

"I'll play the piano."

Cassie whirled around. "Rafe! I didn't hear you come in."

"I know. You've been busy." He uncoiled his long body from the wooden auditorium chair. "Do you need me?"

Of course she needed him, just to breathe, to live, to be happy. "But you once told me you could only play fraternity songs on the piano."

She'd remembered! Rafe thought. That warmed him as nothing had in the two weeks since the brawl at Owney's. He'd been sleeping in the guest room to give her space, and he missed her more every day. "I'm not as well trained or as proficient as you or Cosmo—"

"Cosmo's dead," a youngster piped up. "We're sorry. We liked him."

Rafe smiled. "So did I." He glanced at his wife. "I can read music and play with some proficiency. My mother thought it was the mark of a superior person to be versed in the arts. Even though I can't recall that my playing did much more than annoy her."

Cassie was sure none of the children noticed the thinly veiled sarcasm, the irony in his voice. Yet she heard a softness there, an acceptance, not bitterness.

It pained her to imagine him as a young boy laboring over his piano lessons, perhaps believing that he could impress the parents he rarely saw. At what age did he realize that he could never impress them, because his presence was too insignificant to them?

"Well, I could use your help." She almost crumpled when she saw the surprised pleasure flash across his features. She loved him so much, wanted him more each day. Could their life gel so that they could have each other?

He sat down at the old upright and ran his hands over the keys. "It's in tune, but barely."

She shrugged. "Tuning the piano isn't in the budget this year."

"I could cover it."

She stared at him in surprise, then nodded in agreement. Rafe exhaled in relief. She would let him do something for her, and he needed to do anything that would bind them closer. He needed her. She was all of life, all of love for him. Quickly he let his gaze rove her body. She was rounding out in the middle, barely noticeable, but he knew that form better than his own, and he could see it. She excited him, but it was more than passion. It was a monumental love, a need to care for her, to cherish her.

Cassie picked up her baton, studying her pupils as they took up their instruments and waited, poised for her downstroke. She glanced at Rafe, who was scanning the music. When he looked up at her, she tapped her metal music stand twice, raised the baton, then brought it down on the downbeat of a song from a Broadway show. The spring concert would include a selection of show tunes, and the children already loved them. Cassie felt it was healthy for them to study the contemporaries as well as the old masters.

They led off with the poignantly beautiful love song. The pulsating fervor of the piano added just the right verve, and the children not only responded to it, they became part of it. The melody soared and vibrated. Cassie could feel it in her middle, her heart beating in time to the music.

When the song ended, no one moved. The children eyed her, and she stared back at them.

"You know you did that well," she said at last, "that you've never done it better. How did it feel?"

"Great."

"Good."

"Fantastic."

The hearty comments made them laugh. Cassie laughed with them. They were an orchestra.

Rafe watched her as the children shouted out their pleasure. She'd evoked a great response from them. She'd made them a part of music. They'd remember that in years to come. So would he. When she finally turned to him, so did the children. He found that he was holding his breath.

"And you were very good, too, Mr. Brockman," Cassie said. "We might even make you a permanent member of our orchestra." She smiled when he rose to his feet and gave a deep impresario's bow. Her smile widened when the children hooted with laughter. It'd been good to have him there, and the children had enjoyed it.

"I'd be honored to be among such an august company," he said solemnly.

"What does a-gust mean?" one boy asked. "Is that a wind?"

"That's a pretty accurate assessment of what I said," Rafe answered. "But august means worthy of respect or awe."

Cassie was on the verge of asking Rafe to rehearse another piece with them, when a girl's voice sounded from behind her.

"Mrs. Brockman, are you ready for us?"

Cassie spun around. Three of her music students were there for their lesson. Her gaze flew to the clock. Rafe had been with them for half an hour! It had seemed like five minutes. "Ah, excuse me, children," she said to the orchestra. "You must get to your class. The bell will be ringing in a few seconds."

Squeals and yelps accompanied this announcement, and there was great scrambling for books and bags and such. Pencils and pens flew and were retrieved as they stampeded from the auditorium.

Then the room was quiet, and the three new students stared at Rafe with unashamed curiosity.

"Beth, Dillon, Geord, this is—"

"We know who it is," Beth Mills said eagerly. "He's your husband." She looked at the others. "They're going to have a baby. My mother said so." She turned back to Rafe. "My mother says that you'd better have a good job. Children are expensive. Have you got a job?"

"Beth, I think it's time for your lesson—"

"Indeed I have a job, Beth," Rafe said. "I'm in real estate, and I have other business interests. In fact, I'm moving more and more of my work to

Alaska." He looked at Cassie. "From now on I'll have to go to New York only about once a month, or even every two months."

Cassie looked stunned, but young Beth was dubious. "Why can't you work in Valdez all the time? Are you a drug dealer in New York? I saw men like that on television." She preened in front of her friends, who looked at her blankly.

"Beth!" Cassie said sharply, hoping to curtail one of her most precocious students.

Beth merely sat down and opened her flute case. "My mother says a man should have a decent job."

"Tell your mother I agree with her, Beth," Rafe said solemnly.

"I'll tell her." She started fitting her flute together, and the other two sat down and began doing the same.

Cassie looked at Rafe helplessly.

He tried to smother his amusement, but finally ended up turning his face away.

"Work on your scales," Cassie told her students, then accompanied Rafe to the door of the auditorium. "Sorry about that. Beth is a little outspoken."

"Is that what we have to look forward to?" Mirth bubbled over, and he laughed.

Happiness spurted through her. It was the first time that Rafe had mentioned the baby in such a way. She pressed her hand over her middle. "I suppose. Girls can be very gabby."

"I hope we have a girl." He reached out and put his hand over hers.

Cassie was breathless, her vocal cords frozen.

"Good-bye, darling. See you tonight." He kissed her mouth, his lips lingering there.

When he turned away, her voice uncorked itself. "Did you mean that about going to New York only once a month?"

He turned and nodded. "Little by little I'm weaning the business away from there and adding to it up here."

"Good."

"I hope you mean that."

"I do."

"See ya," he whispered, and disappeared out the door.

Cassie stared at the swinging door for long moments until Beth's determined off-key playing drew her attention.

When Cassie left the school that afternoon, she noted happily how bright and strong the sunshine was. The worst of winter might be over.

"Cassie."

She turned. "Willie. What are you doing here?"

He took her arm and walked with her to her car. "I took a chance you'd still be here and that you'd give me a ride to the house."

"What happened to your truck?"

He shrugged. "It died."

"Where were you?" She started the engine, then drove across the parking lot and out to the street.

"The hatchery. We opened today."

"What?" Her hands jerked on the wheel, almost sending them into the opposite lane. A blare of horns admonished her.

"Hey, Cass. Let me drive, will you?"

"Don't be silly. I'm fine. Now, tell me what you said, and if you're kidding."

He shook his head. "Not kidding. We opened today and hired ten men—"

"Ten? You can't do that. Where will we get the money for wages?"

"Rafe. He's backing us."

The car swerved again.

"Hell, Cass, you'll pile us up."

Ignoring his warning, she glared at a driver who was honking furiously. "Take a dive, you jerk. Now, Willie, tell me about Rafe."

"I'll tell you nothing until you pull over and let me drive," her brother said.

Knowing how stubborn he could be, she put on her signal and pulled to the side of the road.

Willie got out, and she slid over to the passenger side. "Now, tell me," she said as he slid behind the wheel.

He grimaced as he had to press the accelerator nearly to the floor in order to get the car moving. "This heap isn't much better than mine."

"It runs. Tell me, Willie."

"It seems your husband made up his mind to get in the fishing business. I guess he and Dad have been talking about it for months. On his last trip to New York, Rafe was able to line up solid investing from some of his colleagues."

"Daddy never said anything." Neither had Rafe, she thought, but that wasn't surprising. He could be secretive when he chose. She had proof of that. She felt a shading of sadness, then could've kicked herself. It didn't matter whether everything was perfect. She knew life without Rafe was no life at all.

"I guess Dad was waiting until he was sure it would work. Not wanting to get our hopes up, just in case it all fell through, you know."

Cassie nodded absently, and Willie went on, "Since you're eating with us tonight, I'll drive us to the house, and you can call Rafe to meet us there."

"No! Drive me home, then you and I can drive back with Rafe." She wanted a few minutes alone with Rafe before they were surrounded by her family.

Willie grimaced but nodded.

Rafe must have seen them driving up, for he was running out of the house before Willie had even stopped. He hurried to the car and wrenched open her door. "What's wrong? Why is Willie driving you?" He all but lifted her out of the car, cuddling her close.

Willie got out and leaned on the roof of the car, his laughter puffing out in clouds into the frosty air of March. "Nothing's wrong. My truck broke down, and I hitched a ride with Cass. Get in, and we'll go back to the house. I'm starved."

Rafe studied Cassie for a long moment, then looked at Willie. "You drive the car, Willie, and keep it until your truck is fixed. I'll drive Cassie to work until her new one comes." He grinned at her surprise. "It's a new sport utility vehicle, four-wheel drive, floor shift. It'll go anywhere, snow, rain, whatever."

Willie whistled softly, then got back into the car. "I'm looking for a wife like you, Rafe," he shouted as he drove off.

"Chucklehead," Rafe said.

Cassie leaned against him. "You're a nut, Rafe Brockman."

"I'm a nut about you, Cassie Brockman." He turned and led her into the house, closing the door behind them.

When she was about to go up the stairs, he held on to her arm.

"What is it?"

He grinned. "I enjoyed buying that new vehicle for you."

Cassie blinked. Was she looking at a boy excited by the Christmas season, or a cool, calculating businessman who'd managed to add great portions of platinum real estate to his coffers? A boy, to be sure. And she loved that facet of him. "I don't think I'll ever give you anything so grand."

"You already have. You married me."

There was no hint of humor in his eyes.

She swallowed. "That's a nice thing to say." Nice? It was wonderful.

"It's true."

Impulsively she reached out and touched his face. "How did our love last through the years, Rafe? That's what I find so incomprehensible. With all that was between us, how could it stay alive, still burn hot?"

"I've often wondered myself."

"But it did survive, didn't it?"

He slipped his arm around her waist and led her up the stairs. "I can answer for me. Yes." At the top of the stairs he turned to the bedroom. "Do you want to change before we go?"

"I'd like to. We haven't that much time, though."

"Right. If we're a minute late, those brothers of yours clear the table of food."

"Big appetites. Nordstroms are noted for them."

"Nordstrom. It's a lovely name." He followed her

into the bedroom. "I never asked you if you'd prefer to keep it."

She shrugged. "I like my name, but I like Brockman too. How would it be if we named one of our children Nordstrom?" She deliberately spoke of "children," plural, and noted the panic that flashed across his face. Then it was gone, and he smiled easily.

"It's a great middle name for a girl, or first name for a boy. But we were discussing something else before we came in here."

"Our love."

"Yes."

"Sit down, Cassie." He waited until she'd settled herself on the bed, then said, "That day you called me from the airport and said that you and Cosmo were going to Alaska, I couldn't get my breath. I think I have some idea about what it feels like to have a heart attack, Cass. I don't know how long I sat there, dying. Then my secretary reminded me of a meeting in five minutes. I went to the meeting, came back and dictated some letters, called London and Le Havre and talked to our European associates, then went home and got roaring drunk on some Scotch I'd bought for just that purpose. The next morning I barely remembered anything that had happened the day before—except that you were gone."

Cassie nodded, staring across the room at the old-fashioned triangular-shaped fireplace in the far corner. "I didn't get drunk, but I didn't know where I was. Cosmo kept trying to comfort me, and I wanted to be comforted, but I felt as though I'd dismembered myself. No circulation to the heart, to the limbs . . . to my soul." She looked up at him, her smile twisted. "I couldn't seem to thaw out. I'd start shivering, and yet I knew I wasn't that cold. I was on shutdown."

"After a time I got working again," Rafe said. "I flew to Europe, Asia, Africa, at the drop of a hat. I went helicopter skiing in Nepal. A private good-old-boys club set it up. Dangerous as hell. The others thought it a great adventure. I had to fight a catatonic boredom. I was going to hell in a hand basket. All I knew was that I had to find a way to convince you I was necessary to your life."

"You were."

"And you were my life's blood."

She held her hand out to him. "Why were we so slow?"

"I don't know. Cosmo got after both of us."

They smiled, but the smiles were tinged with sadness.

"We could've lost," Cassie said at last, her pent-up fear spilling out. "Even with Cosmo we—"

"I know, I know." He threaded his fingers with hers. "I've thought of that many times. I can't say I've ever subscribed to a theory of predestination . . . but I do believe we had some outside help in this, wife."

"I've thought that more than once. And I'm grateful."

"So am I, so am I."

In companionable silence they gazed at each other.

Was there a smiling spirit at their side?

Supper at the Nordstroms was the usual hearty fare. That night it was a family favorite of baked salmon with dill sauce, red potatoes boiled in their skins, then broiled lightly with olive oil, hot broccoli-and-carrot salad, and lots of warm oatmeal bread. Flaky apple and blueberry pies with clotted cream finished the wonderful meal.

"He's beginning to eat like the boys," Mary said to Cassie as she happily watched Rafe polish off his second serving of pie.

Cassie smiled at her mother. "He loves your cooking." She turned to her father. "So, Dad, tell me about this new fishing venture you and Rafe have."

Willie groaned.

Kort and Lars glared at him, while Helborg winced.

Rafe paused with a forkful of apple pie halfway to his mouth. "Honey, I was going to tell you when you came home after school—"

"Which day?"

"I just wanted to make sure everything was going to be settled. There was more than one offer in on the hatchery, and it's taken all these months to negotiate the deal."

"You could've told me," Cassie said quietly.

"And me," Mary said, eyeing her spouse.

"And me," Linnie added, staring at Kort.

"Now, Linnie, honey—"

"And me," Adela interjected. "I want to invest."

"I could too," Linnie said.

"So could I," Cassie said. "I have three hundred dollars in the bank."

Her husband smiled. "That's not necessary, Cassie. I'm backing this all the way."

Helborg nodded, then looked at Mary. "It wasn't easy for me to take Rafe's money," he said by way of explanation. "But I don't mind now, because I've made him my full partner."

Willie whooped. Standing, he walked around the table to Rafe and lifted him clean out of his chair. "I know you wouldn't like it if I lifted Cassie in her condition. So you're it."

Rafe laughed with the rest.

Nine

Rafe and Cassie were silent as they drove home from the Nordstroms'.

Rafe had been sure she would want to talk. That she said nothing made him uneasy. In another lifetime he would've taken the silence in stride, relaxed in their cocoon of togetherness. Now, he took nothing for granted.

He drove into the garage, then hurried around to help Cassie from the car.

"That was good of you to lend Willie my car," she said. "I should've thought of it myself."

He leaned down and pulled her up into his arms. "Not lend, gave. Yours will be coming very soon." He turned to the door.

"I can walk."

"I like to carry you." He managed the door out of the garage but fumbled the one into the kitchen. Giggling, Cassie ended up opening it.

He strode into the kitchen, frowning down at

her. "You shouldn't be laughing at me. I'm showing you my Superman side."

"It's sagging." Laughter pealed out of her.

Rafe's heart beat out of rhythm. This was the way it had been when they'd first lived together. Cassie had been so carefree, so happy. He wanted her that way always. But he'd let his dark side blight their togetherness. He wasn't bitter about the time they'd been apart, but it still made him angry at himself to think that he'd let it happen. Now, he could've jeopardized their relationship again . . . with a business deal with her father. Dammit to hell! Would he never learn? He let her slide down his body. "I didn't want to hide things from you. It was just my business wariness getting in the way. Do you believe that?"

"Yes." She was getting to know this man of hers. Mostly she was beginning to accept just how much he loved her, and how great his struggle was to get away from the dark, hidden side of his personality. Every day she saw small changes in him. She knew he loved her. The battle he was winning to be more open with her was an unmistakable demonstration of that. "I've always known you were a man of great strength, Rafe. In these last two months I've seen more and more manifestations of that." She rubbed her hand over his cheek, delighting in the new bristles that'd already begun to form.

Rafe felt warmed to his soul. "Always know that I love you, Cassie."

She nodded. "And always know that I love you, Rafe."

He kissed her gently, his heart thudding against

his ribs. "You give me peace and joy, and excite the hell out of me."

She laughed.

"Shall I get you a hot drink?"

"No, I'm going right to my room."

He hid his disappointment behind a smile. "Right. I'll talk to you tomorrow."

"Right." She turned and left.

Whistling tunelessly Rafe opened and shut the refrigerator doors, ignoring everything. He wasn't hungry for food, just for Cassie. Finally he poured himself a glass of milk, then went upstairs to his room down the hall from hers. A cold shower. Just what he needed.

Standing under the shower, his skin goose-bumping from the cold water, he closed his eyes and held his face upward.

"Yikes! It's too cold. Turn on the warm."

Rafe's eyes snapped open and immediately flooded with water. He swallowed it, too, and started coughing as he tried to see. She was there . . . with him . . . naked. He didn't move. He could only stare at her. "Cassie?"

He swiped at his eyes, staring at her naked body, luminescent with the reflections of light and the pearling of water. Passion roared through him. His mouth was dry even as he was being deluged with water. "Cassie?"

"Yes." She reached around him, adjusting the water temperature to warm. "I was wondering how you'd feel about moving up the date for the end of our agreement. Say . . . today, for instance. What do you think?"

"As long as we live together."

"Of course."

"Great," he said hoarsely. He reached out, then pulled back.

She took his hand and put it on her breasts. "I was thinking we might celebrate."

"You're—you're pregnant."

"Pregnant, not incapacitated." She leaned against him, wriggling her body. "This pregnant lady feels very sexy."

"Only if it's safe." He reeled with the power of her. Her heat had set him on fire. Like an automaton he reached for soap and water and laved her gently. "I burn for you, my Cassiopeia, but I won't endanger you."

"You're being silly." She dragged his head down and pressed her mouth to his.

Rafe dropped the cloth and soap, his hands coming to grasp her waist. "Darling," he said against her mouth. "I love you."

"And I love you." She knew they'd have problems down through the years, but they'd face them one at a time, face them and defeat them.

"Don't ever leave me," Rafe murmured in her ear.

"I won't." When his mouth scored down her face to her neck, she tilted her head back to give him freer access.

Cupping her buttocks with his hands, he lifted her against him. "You drive me wild."

"Show me."

Her sultry voice almost unmanned him, and he slipped as he stepped out of the shower. Catching himself, he shot her a worried look.

"I'm fine, Rafe, and not made of cobwebs. I'm Alaskan, remember."

"Yeah." He dried her carefully, then ran the

towel quickly over himself. He was so hot for her, he could've exploded, but he was still cautious. He carried her through to the bedroom, placing her on the bed and going down beside her. "Swear that this is all right for you."

"I swear," she told him solemnly. She pressed her hand to his cheek. "I like your face, Rafe. I hope our baby looks like you."

Unrestrained pleasure flowed like a river through him. "Darling," he groaned, lowering his head to her breasts. He began kissing her. Her fire was there, lighting his; he could feel all the yearnings of his life reaching out to this one tempestuous, compassionate, happy woman, and he gave his emotions full rein. "No, no. I want our baby to look like you." He lifted his head. "I remember the first time I saw you."

"When I put my flute between your legs and jarred you a bit."

"I was jarred by you, not the flute . . . and aroused. And that knocked me out. I was looking down at a Christmas elf, and I was mad about you. I had a forty-five-minute ride to the airport, everything was stowed in the limo for my trip to Europe, then there you were, and all my plans went to hell."

She curled her arms around him. "Love me, Rafe."

Together they climbed the lover's mountain, peaking in a cataclysmic explosion of giving, loving, and want.

"I'll never give you up, Cassie."

"I'll never let you," she promised sleepily, happily curled into his body. All the fears that had plagued her were slipping away, and she was glad to see the last of them. They were together, where they belonged. She tightened her hold and drifted into happy sleep.

What woke her she didn't know, but she reached out, eyes still closed, for her husband. When she felt nothing, she came fully awake. Sitting up, she looked around. He was standing by the window, statue-still, gazing out as though he were in secret communication with the snowy outdoors. "Rafe?"

He turned slowly, his face shadowed. "Sorry, darling. I didn't mean to waken you."

"You were gone. I woke," she said absently. Even in the darkened room she could tell he was tense. "You haven't slept."

"I've been thinking."

"Can you share your thoughts?"

He moved toward the bed. "Boring stuff, but I'll tell you."

She could hear the bitter amusement in his voice. "But it's hurtful, too, isn't it?"

"Not as much now," he said softly.

She felt the bed give as he climbed in beside her, then his arms slid around her. She was relieved that he wanted to hold her. Their relationship still had its fragile moments, and she wanted to do all she could to protect it. "Tell me," she whispered against his neck.

"I was thinking about when I worked in the company when I'd come home from boarding school for the holidays. My father really didn't care about me learning the business, but Uncle Edward was a bear about it. He thought the real estate business in Manhattan was the only way to go, and he was good at it."

Cassie said nothing, quite sure Rafe was skimming the perimeter of his tale.

He swallowed. "One day—"

At the long pause, his deep breaths loud in the stillness, she hugged him. "If it's too difficult—"

"No, no, it isn't that. . . . Yes, I suppose it is that, in a way. But I want you to know, Cass. I want no more barriers between us."

"Then tell me."

"One day I was carting letters to the mailroom. I passed the entrance to the executive lounge and heard my mother's voice. Normally you wouldn't hear people talking in there because of the way the room was constructed. But her voice was raised, agitated. I stopped. I guess I was going to greet her . . . I don't know. A short hall led to the suite of rooms. You made a left and then a right to get to the main room." He inhaled. "We've since moved out of that building to a newer, larger one."

"I see."

He chuckled. "That I'm hedging?"

"Yes." She pressed her mouth to his neck.

"I turned the first corner and was more or less isolated from the outside corridor, and from them. As I was about to round the next corner and speak to my mother, I heard Uncle Edward's voice. Though he spoke in a lower tone, there was no mistaking his anger."

Cassie froze, suddenly wondering if she did want to hear this.

"He told her to leave," Rafe went on, "that he had no interest in what she intended, that he loved his wife and always would."

Cassie gasped.

"Yes. My mother was trying to seduce my uncle, or so it seemed to me then." He paused, his hold tightening on Cassie. "Once more he told her to leave, and he said that the only thing she had that interested him was her children, and that he didn't see how she could be so blind to her good fortune in being a parent to such children. He called us precious."

"And so you are."

"Thank you, darling."

He laughed briefly, but when he continued his tone was flat, as though he were reading from a text.

"She said she'd see him in hell before he got us, that Linnie and I meant nothing to her except as passports to financial independence, but she'd see to it that they would be out of his life and Adela's. My uncle shouted at her then. And she cursed him."

Cassie looked up at him through the gray darkness. "Then you left?"

"Yes." His hands tightened on her. "It was strange. I suppose I'd always known that Aunt Adela and Uncle Edward loved us as parents, and that my mother and father didn't have that capacity. But it hurt like hell to hear it like that."

"Some of it might have been temper."

"I've thought of that. And I'm sure that was true to an extent. But I'm also sure that my mother was a woman who should've remained childless." He reached up and turned on the light over their bed. "But I understand her better since meeting you."

"What do you mean?"

"I've always thought of my mother as a manipulative woman, a greedy woman who always wanted more. But in the years that you and I were apart, I began to see her differently."

"How?"

"If she truly loved my uncle and couldn't have him, that could've soured her. I know how strong love can be, how entwining great passion is. Once it's experienced, it can be like dying of thirst to be without it. Even the soul shrivels."

"And you think they shared that grand passion?" Cassie was surprised. "You know, I'm not sure that would've been my guess, but now that you mention it . . ." She searched his face. "Are you sure your uncle didn't—"

"If you could've seen my uncle with Adela, you would've known how it was between them. They used to laugh all the time, and they were always touching, kissing. And they treated us the same way. It was hard for me to show my feelings, but my aunt and uncle were very open with their affection. When Linnie and I were with them, we'd be happy."

"Oh, Rafe, then you did have a wonderful mother and father. You just happened to call them uncle and aunt."

"Yes." He was silent for a minute, then said, "If my mother had tried to get my uncle . . . if she had children just to ensure my uncle's interest . . ." He shook his head.

"We won't ever know. But does it matter? You're dealing with it."

"Yes. My wife taught me many things."

"Your wife thinks you're pretty smart on your own." She reached up and kissed his cheek. "You've started to forgive your mother."

"I think I have . . . completely." He shook his head. "But what a waste their lives were."

"They might've been different when they were younger. If your parents were heavy drinkers, took drugs . . ."

"And they did," he said grimly.

"That changes the personality. She and your father might've been quite different had they not been addicted to such mind-bending, emotion-damaging chemicals."

Rafe kissed her hair. "I've thought of that, too, Cass, and I can accept it now. Before we met, I buried it all. But the harder I pushed it away, the more it stayed a part of me. I felt bitter. I don't now."

She hugged him, feeling a rush of love. "You've won, Rafe."

He nodded. "And one day soon I'm going to talk to Linnie about our parents, share what I've told you. If Mother loved Edward all that time, she must've been in terrible pain."

"And your father must've guessed about some of it."

"Lord, I don't ever want to be so unhappy."

"You won't be. I promise."

Ten

Pregnancy was no picnic, but Cassie didn't find it that difficult. She was supported by her mother and father, Adela, her sisters, Linnie, and even Buster Dunn. He had stayed in New York to take care of Rafe's apartment, but when Rafe had told him Cassie was pregnant, Buster had packed and taken the first flight out—without even bothering to tell Rafe. Rafe had been nonplussed when Buster arrived on their doorstep, but Cassie had been delighted. At the very least, she told Adela, Buster should help *Rafe* get through the pregnancy. Every time she looked around, he was there, a sickly smile on his face.

"If you're trying to reassure me, Rafe Brockman," she told him during her sixth month, "you aren't. There's nothing wrong with me, and there's no reason you shouldn't go to New York this week. Linnie says—"

"What does she know? She's never been pregnant," he groused, watching her like a hawk.

"Go to New York."

"No. Kort and Linnie will take care of things there."

"It's your business," Cassie said. "And I think it would be best for all concerned—"

"You're my business," he interrupted. "I have to take care of you."

"I think I'll end up taking care of you."

"Don't be silly."

One night during her eighth month they dined at her parents' house.

The family watched Rafe, not her.

"He looks like he's going to explode," Asty said from the side of her mouth.

"Astrid," her mother said warningly.

"Well, he does. What's wrong with him, Cass?"

"Pregnant," Cassie said, resignedly.

Her sister stared at her, then leaned over and whispered something to Andy.

Titters began as the whispers went around the table.

No matter how Mary shushed them, Cassie's siblings didn't let up.

Rafe seemed impervious to their jibes. "Laugh all you want. Wait until you're pregnant."

Even Helborg joined in the guffaws. Mary's stern looks had become smothered amusement.

Rafe looked sheepish for a moment, then went right back to being concerned about his wife.

When Cassie rose from the table, he was on his feet in a flash. "What's wrong?"

"I'm going to the bathroom."

"Oh. I'll go with you."

"I'm fine."

He nodded. "I'll wait outside the door."

Cassie rolled her eyes at her mother.

"I hope he survives this," Mary whispered to Adela when they were cutting the pie for dessert.

"I think it's wonderful," Adela said. "I've never seen him so happy . . . or so petrified."

The baby girl came three weeks early and almost frightened her father to death.

"It's not time," Rafe said hoarsely as he helped his wife into the car. "And where the hell is Buster? Why did he have to go grocery-shopping now?"

Cassie didn't bother to answer. She was bent almost double with a sudden pain.

"Dammit, dammit! This isn't by the book," Rafe muttered, hunched over the wheel, blowing his horn as he weaved through the traffic. "And babies come at night, not during rush hour."

"I'll remember to mention that to our progeny right after birth," Cassie said, then gasped at another pain.

"Dammit, Cassie, are you all right? The books say you should be relaxed and breathing through your mouth."

"And you've read everything ever written on the subject."

"Someone had to," he said, then put his hand on her protectively as he took the last corner on two wheels.

"Slow down." Cassie was uncomfortable, but she felt like laughing too. Her husband was parchment white. "You should've let me drive."

"Cassie! Sometimes your humor is out of place."

"Sorry."

The attendants took care of Cassie and Rafe at the emergency door.

"I'll carry her," Rafe said.

"We'll push her," a nurse answered. "You can walk next to her."

Rafe looked mulish, then complied when Cassie had another pain.

It almost took longer to cap and gown Rafe than it did to prep Cassie. He wouldn't be budged from his wife, nor would he take his eyes off her.

Dr. Anderson leaned over and whispered to Cassie. She laughed, then gasped when another pain hit her. Rafe looked as if he was going to faint.

"Take it easy, Daddy," Dr. Anderson said calmly.

"Why is she in pain?"

"She's having a baby. There will be some discomfort."

Rafe opened his mouth, but his wife forestalled him.

"Rafe, put on your gown."

He did.

The entire family was in the waiting room, including Buster. The family doctor had been out twice to talk to them.

"I think Dr. Anderson's going to kick Rafe out of the hospital," Willie said. "Here she comes again, Mother."

Dr. Anderson stopped in front of them, harassed and red-faced. "Mrs. Nordstrom, can't you do something with your son-in-law? He's disturbing the birthing room, and he's threatened to sue me and the nurses."

"Oh, dear, Doctor, I am sorry. But he's been so worried about Cassie."

Adela chuckled, earning a frown from the physician. "I'm sorry, but I can't help it. He's been driving all of us crazy for almost nine months."

"Now, he's driving us crazy in the birthing room."

"Try to understand, Doctor," Mary said. "He's so in love with Cassie, and he's worried that something could happen."

"Crazy, that's what he is." Dr. Anderson sighed, then turned and headed back to the birthing room.

Lars stared at Kort, who was watching Linnie closely. "I hope you're not going to threaten to tear down the hospital, little brother, when your turn comes."

"We might adopt," Kort said.

"No, we won't," Linnie said.

Lars laughed. "Don't argue, little brother. It never worked for Rafe."

Kort looked worried.

Linnie patted his hand.

In the birthing room, masked and gowned, Rafe ignored the sweat rolling down his face like rain as he watched his wife in the last throes of labor. Cassie. Cassie. It hurt her so. He wished it was his pain.

The baby's wail and Cassie's breathy, hiccupy

laugh sent him to his knees next to her. "Darling?"

"Look at the baby."

"I can't turn my head," he mumbled.

"Now, he gets weak," Dr. Anderson muttered, laying the infant on the mother's chest. "There's your daughter, Cass."

"Isn't she beautiful, Rafe? Darling? What is it?"

Eyes streaming tears, he lifted a shaking hand and touched the baby, then his wife. "I—I never knew we could have someone so beautiful. I love you, Cassie." He leaned over his wife and child, shaken to his soul.

"And I love you." She cuddled his head close to her.

Dr. Anderson looked at the nurse who'd assisted her, her eyes suspiciously moist. "Sometimes I love this job."

"And he loves them," the nurse murmured, nodding her head toward Rafe. She patted the shoulder of the happy father. "I think Mrs. Brockman did just fine, not just in birthing, but picking out the right man."

"I agree," Cassie said.

"Will you miss not having Christmas in Manhattan?" Cassie asked her husband on Christmas Eve. He was holding their daughter, Mary Adela, while he put some presents under the tree. When Rafe was home, he was usually holding, or feeding, or just watching, the baby. He'd become wonderfully adept at washing, changing, and dressing their daughter.

Rafe looked at her, taken aback. "Are you serious? I love it here. You know that." He grinned, wondering how there could be such happiness. Fatherhood was the most delightful thing that had happened to him, except for being Cassie's husband. "Of course, I'll always have wonderful memories of Manhattan. And I thought we'd go together in January sometime. We could see some shows, visit the restaurants we always liked. Maybe do some ice-skating."

She smiled and nodded. "We could do that."

"We could even do some skiing in the Adirondacks."

"And you could show me how good you are."

"That's the idea. Always trying to impress my lady."

"How about Maddy?" Cassie used the love name Mary Adela's grandfather had given her.

"I'm going to give her two grandmothers a crack at her. They've been dying to get rid of us so they could care for her."

Cassie chuckled. "Aren't Adela and Mom funny?"

"Yes," Rafe said, cuddling his daughter and murmuring love words.

"You're funnier."

He glanced at her, smiling. "She's beautiful like her mother. And I'm crazy about her."

He held out his free arm to her, and she snuggled close to him, closing her eyes and feeling the familiar heat and serene sense of security.

"I love you, Cassie mine. You've made my life."

"And you've made mine."

He looked up at the tall Christmas tree, then whispered in her ear, "'Twas the night before Christmas . . .'"

Cassie's heart bubbled over with love. "I remember."

"So do I." He kissed her gently, and outside the window, soft snow fell as Alaska preened herself in her mantle of white.

THE EDITOR'S CORNER

What could be more romantic than Valentine's Day and six LOVESWEPT romances all in one glorious month! Celebrate this special time of the year by cuddling up with the wonderful books coming your way soon.

The first of our reading treasures is **ANGELS SINGING** by Joan Elliott Pickart, LOVESWEPT #594. Drew Sloan's first impression of Memory Lawson isn't the best, considering she's pointing a shotgun at him and accusing him of trespassing on her mountain. But the heat that flashes between them convinces him to stay and storm the walls around her heart . . . until she believes that she's just the kind of warm, loving woman he's been looking for. Joan comes through once more with a winning romance!

We have a real treat in store for fans of Kay Hooper. After a short hiatus for work on **THE DELANEY CHRISTMAS CAROL** and other books, Kay returns with **THE TOUCH OF MAX,** LOVESWEPT #595, the *fiftieth* book in her illustrious career! If you were a fan of Kay's popular "Hagan Strikes Again" and "Once Upon a Time" series, you'll be happy to know that **THE TOUCH OF MAX** is the first of four "Men of Mysteries Past" books, all of which center around Max Bannister's priceless gem collection, which the police are using as bait to catch a notorious thief. But when innocent Dinah Layton gets tangled in the trap, it'll take that special touch of Max to set her free . . . and capture her heart. A sheer delight—and it'll have you breathlessly waiting for more. Welcome back, Kay!

In Charlotte Hughes's latest novel, Crescent City's new soccer coach is **THE INCREDIBLE HUNK,** LOVE-SWEPT #596. Utterly male, gorgeously virile, Jason Profitt has the magic touch with kids. What more perfect guy could there be for a redhead with five children to raise! But Maggie Farnsworth is sure that once he's seen her chaotic life, he'll run for the hills. Jason has another plan of action in mind, though—to make a home in her loving arms. Charlotte skillfully blends humor and passion in this page-turner of a book.

Appropriately enough, Marcia Evanick's contribution to the month, **OVER THE RAINBOW,** LOVESWEPT #597, is set in a small town called Oz, where neither Hillary Walker nor Mitch Ferguson suspects his kids of matchmaking when he's forced to meet the lovely speech teacher. The plan works so well the kids are sure they'll get a mom for Christmas. But Hillary has learned never to trust her heart again, and only Mitch's passionate persuasion can change her mind. You can count on Marcia to deliver a fun-filled romance.

A globetrotter in buckskins and a beard, Nick Leclerc has never considered himself **THE FOREVER MAN,** LOVESWEPT #598, by Joan J. Domning. Yet when he appears in Carla Hudson's salon for a haircut and a shave, her touch sets his body on fire and fills him with unquenchable longing. The sexy filmmaker has leased Carla's ranch to uncover an ancient secret, but instead he finds newly awakened dreams of hearth and home. Joan will capture your heart with this wonderful love story.

Erica Spindler finishes this dazzling month with **TEMPT-ING CHANCE,** LOVESWEPT #599. Shy Beth Waters doesn't think she has what it takes to light the sensual spark in gorgeous Chance Michaels. But the outrageous results of her throwing away a chain letter finally convince her that she's woman enough to tempt Chance—and that he's more than eager to be caught in her embrace. Humorous, yet seething with emotion and desire, **TEMPTING CHANCE** is one tempting morsel from talented Erica.

Look for four spectacular novels on sale now from FANFARE. Award-winning Iris Johansen confirms her place as a major star with **THE TIGER PRINCE,** a magnificent new historical romance that sweeps from exotic realms to the Scottish highlands. In a locked room of shadows and sandalwood, Jane Barnaby meets adventurer Ruel McClaren and is instantly transformed from a hard-headed businesswoman to the slave of a passion she knows she must resist.

Suzanne Robinson first introduced us to Blade in **LADY GALLANT,** and now in the new thrilling historical romance **LADY DEFIANT,** Blade returns as a bold, dashing hero. One of Queen Elizabeth's most dangerous spies, he must romance a beauty named Oriel who holds a clue that could change history. Desire builds and sparks fly as these two unwillingly join forces to thwart a deadly conspiracy.

Hailed by Katherine Stone as "emotional, compelling, and triumphant!", **PRIVATE SCANDALS** is the debut novel by very talented Christy Cohen. From the glamour of New York to the glitter of Hollywood comes a heartfelt story of scandalous desires and long-held secrets . . . of dreams realized and longings denied . . . of three remarkable women whose lifelong friendship would be threatened by one man.

Available once again is **A LOVE FOR ALL TIME** by bestselling author Dorothy Garlock. In this moving tale, Casey Farrow gives up all hope of a normal life when a car crash leaves indelible marks on her breathtaking beauty . . . until Dan Farrow, the man who rescued her from the burning vehicle, convinces her that he loves her just the way she is.

Also on sale this month in the hardcover edition from Doubleday is **THE LADY AND THE CHAMP** by Fran Baker. When a former Golden Gloves champion meets an elegant, uptown girl, the result is a stirring novel of courageous love that Julie Garwood has hailed as "unforgettable."

Happy reading!

With warmest wishes,

Nita Taublib

Nita Taublib
Associate Publisher
LOVESWEPT and FANFARE

OFFICIAL RULES TO WINNERS CLASSIC SWEEPSTAKES

No Purchase necessary. To enter the sweepstakes follow instructions found elsewhere in this offer. You can also enter the sweepstakes by hand printing your name, address, city, state and zip code on a 3" x 5" piece of paper and mailing it to: Winners Classic Sweepstakes, P.O. Box 785, Gibbstown, NJ 08027. Mail each entry separately. Sweepstakes begins 12/1/91. Entries must be received by 6/1/93. Some presentations of this sweepstakes may feature a deadline for the Early Bird prize. If the offer you receive does, then to be eligible for the Early Bird prize your entry must be received according to the Early Bird date specified. Not responsible for lost, late, damaged, misdirected, illegible or postage due mail. Mechanically reproduced entries are not eligible. All entries become property of the sponsor and will not be returned.

Prize Selection/Validations: Winners will be selected in random drawings on or about 7/30/93, by VENTURA ASSOCIATES, INC., an independent judging organization whose decisions are final. Odds of winning are determined by total number of entries received. Circulation of this sweepstakes is estimated not to exceed 200 million. Entrants need not be present to win. All prizes are guaranteed to be awarded and delivered to winners. Winners will be notified by mail and may be required to complete an affidavit of eligibility and release of liability which must be returned within 14 days of date of notification or alternate winners will be selected. Any guest of a trip winner will also be required to execute a release of liability. Any prize notification letter or any prize returned to a participating sponsor, Bantam Doubleday Dell Publishing Group, Inc., its participating divisions or subsidiaries, or VENTURA ASSOCIATES, INC. as undeliverable will be awarded to an alternate winner. Prizes are not transferable. No multiple prize winners except as may be necessary due to unavailability, in which case a prize of equal or greater value will be awarded. Prizes will be awarded approximately 90 days after the drawing. All taxes, automobile license and registration fees, if applicable, are the sole responsibility of the winners. Entry constitutes permission (except where prohibited) to use winners' names and likenesses for publicity purposes without further or other compensation.

Participation: This sweepstakes is open to residents of the United States and Canada, except for the province of Quebec. This sweepstakes is sponsored by Bantam Doubleday Dell Publishing Group, Inc. (BDD), 666 Fifth Avenue, New York, NY 10103. Versions of this sweepstakes with different graphics will be offered in conjunction with various solicitations or promotions by different subsidiaries and divisions of BDD. Employees and their families of BDD, its division, subsidiaries, advertising agencies, and VENTURA ASSOCIATES, INC., are not eligible.

Canadian residents, in order to win, must first correctly answer a time limited arithmetical skill testing question. Void in Quebec and wherever prohibited or restricted by law. Subject to all federal, state, local and provincial laws and regulations.

Prizes: The following values for prizes are determined by the manufacturers' suggested retail prices or by what these items are currently known to be selling for at the time this offer was published. Approximate retail values include handling and delivery of prizes. Estimated maximum retail value of prizes: 1 Grand Prize ($27,500 if merchandise or $25,000 Cash); 1 First Prize ($3,000); 5 Second Prizes ($400 each); 35 Third Prizes ($100 each); 1,000 Fourth Prizes ($9.00 each) ; 1 Early Bird Prize ($5,000); Total approximate maximum retail value is $50,000. Winners will have the option of selecting any prize offered at level won. Automobile winner must have a valid driver's license at the time the car is awarded. Trips are subject to space and departure availability. Certain black-out dates may apply. Travel must be completed within one year from the time the prize is awarded. Minors must be accompanied by an adult. Prizes won by minors will be awarded in the name of parent or legal guardian.

For a list of Major Prize Winners (available after 7/30/93): send a self-addressed, stamped envelope entirely separate from your entry to: Winners Classic Sweepstakes Winners, P.O. Box 825, Gibbstown, NJ 08027. Requests must be received by 6/1/93. DO NOT SEND ANY OTHER CORRESPONDENCE TO THIS P.O. BOX.

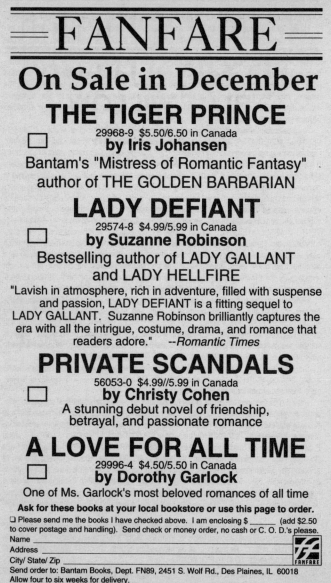

Women's Fiction

On Sale in January

BLUE WILLOW

29690-6 $5.50/6.50 in Canada

by Deborah Smith

Bestselling author of MIRACLE

"Extraordinary talent.... A complex and emotionally wrenching tale that sweeps the readers on an intense rollercoaster ride through the gamut of human emotions." —*Romantic Times*

SINFUL

29312-5 $4.99/5.99 in Canada

by Susan Johnson

Author of FORBIDDEN

"The author's style is a pleasure to read and the love scenes many and lusty!" —*Los Angeles Herald Examiner*

PRINCESS OF THE VEIL

29581-0 $4.99/5.99 in Canada

by Helen Mittermeyer

"Intrigue, a fascinating setting, high adventure, a wonderful love story and steamy sensuality." —*Romantic Times*

LAST SUMMER

56092-1 $4.99//5.99 in Canada

by Theresa Weir

author of FOREVER

A bad-boy actor heads home from Hollywood seeking revenge and runs headlong into love.

FANFARE

The Very Best in Historical Women's Fiction

Rosanne Bittner

_____ 28599-8 EMBERS OF THE HEART $4.50/5.50 in Canada
_____ 28319-7 MONTANA WOMAN $4.99/5.99
_____ 29033-9 IN THE SHADOW OF THE MOUNTAINS $5.50/6.99
_____ 29014-2 SONG OF THE WOLF $4.99/5.99
_____ 29015-0 THUNDER ON THE PLAINS $5.99/6.99

Kay Hooper

_____ 29256-0 THE MATCHMAKER $4.50/5.50

Iris Johansen

_____ 28855-5 THE WIND DANCER $4.95/5.95
_____ 29032-0 STORM WINDS $4.99/5.99
_____ 29244-7 REAP THE WIND $4.99/5.99
_____ 29604-3 THE GOLDEN BARBARIAN $4.99/5.99

Teresa Medeiros

_____ 29047-5 HEATHER AND VELVET $4.99/5.99

Patricia Potter

_____ 29070-3 LIGHTNING $4.99/ 5.99
_____ 29071-1 LAWLESS $4.99/ 5.99
_____ 29069-X RAINBOW $4.99/ 5.99

Fayrene Preston

_____ 29332-X THE SWANSEA DESTINY $4.50/5.50

Amanda Quick

_____ 29325-7 RENDEZVOUS $4.99/5.99
_____ 28354-5 SEDUCTION $4.99/5.99
_____ 28932-2 SCANDAL $4.95/5.95
_____ 28594-7 SURRENDER $4.50/5.50

Deborah Smith

_____ 28759-1 THE BELOVED WOMAN $4.50/ 5.50

Ask for these titles at your bookstore or use this page to order.

Please send me the books I have checked above. I am enclosing $ _____ (add $2.50 to
cover postage and handling). Send check or money order, no cash or C. O. D.'s please.

Mr./ Ms. _____

Address _____

City/ State/ Zip _____

Send order to: Bantam Books, Dept. FN 17, 2451 S. Wolf Road, Des Plaines, IL 60018
Please allow four to six weeks for delivery.

Prices and availability subject to change without notice.   FN 17 - 8/92